"It's not proper, Princess."

"I don't care." Lucia smiled. "My name is Lucia and when we are alone I want you to use it. Being friends will help this process go so much smoother. Besides, it will fit in with your investigation as to my suitability for the throne. So since you want to find out the truth about me, I suggest you spend time with me and judge me for yourself."

"I don't believe that this is necessarily a good idea."

"Why not?"

As Lucia threw the challenge back into his face, he asked himself the same question. Why not? The answer was simple. Lucia Carradigne was as off-limits as a nuclear reactor.

Lucia. He said her name mentally, rolling it silently over his tongue. He could imagine calling her by her name during lovemaking.

He shook his head, clearing it. Lucia may be a touch of heaven, but his job did not include holding it.

Dear Reader,

Welcome to Harlequin American Romance, where our goal is to give you hours of unbeatable reading pleasure.

Kick starting the month is another enthralling installment of THE CARRADIGNES: AMERICAN ROYALTY continuity series. In Michele Dunaway's *The Simply Scandalous Princess*, rumors of a tryst between Princess Lucia Carradigne and a sexy older man leads to the king issuing a royal marriage decree! Follow the series next month in Harlequin Intrigue.

Another terrific romance from Pamela Browning is in store for you with *Rancher's Double Dilemma*. When single dad Garth Colquitt took one look at his new nanny's adorable baby girl, he knew there had to be some kind of crazy mix-up, because his daughter and her daughter were twins! Was a marriage of convenience the solution? Next, don't miss *Help Wanted: Husband?* by Darlene Scarlera. When a single mother-to-be hires a handsome ranch hand, she only has business on her mind. Yet, before long, she wonders if he was just the man she needed—to heal her heart. And rounding out the month is Leah Vale's irresistible debut novel *The Rich Man's Baby*, in which a dashing tycoon discovers he has a son, but the proud mother of his child refuses to let him claim them for his own...unless love enters the equation.

This month, and every month, come home to Harlequin American Romance—and enjoy!

Best,

Melissa Jeglinski
Associate Senior Editor
Harlequin American Romance

THE SIMPLY SCANDALOUS PRINCESS

Michele Dunaway

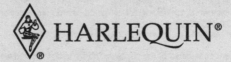

TORONTO • NEW YORK • LONDON
AMSTERDAM • PARIS • SYDNEY • HAMBURG
STOCKHOLM • ATHENS • TOKYO • MILAN • MADRID
PRAGUE • WARSAW • BUDAPEST • AUCKLAND

Special thanks and acknowledgment are given to
Michele Dunaway for her contribution to
THE CARRADIGNES: AMERICAN ROYALTY series.

This book would not have been possible without the following people being the glue that held me together during a particularly rough time:
Will, Pam, Julie, Jenny, Jenni, Charlie and Suzanne.
Thanks to my parents for also being the wind beneath my wings.
You kept me afloat.

To my diamond in the rough—let love polish you.
Always know that I will always
treasure the memories, and that
age never matters in affairs of the heart.

ISBN 0-373-16921-3

THE SIMPLY SCANDALOUS PRINCESS

Visit us at www.eHarlequin.com

Printed in U.S.A.

ABOUT THE AUTHOR

In first grade Michele Dunaway knew she wanted to be a teacher when she grew up, and by second grade she wanted to be an author. By third grade she was determined to be both. Born and raised in a west county suburb of St. Louis, Michele recently moved to five acres in the rolling hills of Labadie. She's traveled extensively, with the cities and places she visits often becoming settings for her stories.

Michele currently teaches high school English, raises her two young daughters and describes herself as a woman who does too much but doesn't want to stop.

Michele loves to hear from readers and you can write to her at P.O. Box 53, Valley Park, MO 63088. Please enclose a SASE.

Books by Michele Dunaway

HARLEQUIN AMERICAN ROMANCE

848—A LITTLE OFFICE ROMANCE
900—TAMING THE TABLOID HEIRESS
921—THE SIMPLY SCANDALOUS PRINCESS

All underlined places are fictitious.

Chapter One

It wasn't necessarily a dirty job, but someone had to do it. As always, Sir Harrison Montcalm, retired general of the Korosol Royal Army, was that man.

He glanced at his watch as he waited for the private elevator that would take him upstairs. One thing he always prided himself on was his punctuality. Never, in all his years of being a trusted adviser, had he been late for a meeting with King Easton, ruler of Korosol.

As Harrison stepped inside the elevator, he brushed off a piece of lint that dared to alight on the left sleeve of his custom navy suit. One other thing Harrison had always prided himself on was his appearance. At forty-five, he still kept his six-foot frame perfectly fit. Now, of course, it took him an extra half hour in the gym to keep trim, and he'd long ago given up worrying or caring anything about the graying temples that graced his dark brown hair.

As the constant companion to the king, Harrison knew his appearance was important. He was nearly always by the king's side. Besides, if a seventy-eight-year-old King Easton could look fifteen years younger, Harrison figured he could too.

He contemplated that as the elevator silently whirred upward.

Not that he'd want to be thirty again. His son Devon would turn thirty in just two years, and Harrison was glad that Devon, a captain of the Royal Guard, hadn't had the wild, careless youth that Harrison had had.

Getting someone pregnant at age seventeen and marrying her out of duty wasn't a life he'd wish on anyone. Then again, duty was all Harrison really knew.

And it was duty, and a loving devotion to King Easton, that drove Harrison. He'd do anything for his king, and that included doing the upcoming job he dreaded. Even taking a bullet for Easton twenty years ago had been easier. He'd simply reacted, loyalty and duty instinctive.

He'd been knighted for his bravery, which had only committed Harrison further into the service of his beloved king.

Harrison glanced at his watch again. For some reason, today the elevator seemed slower than normal. He tapped his forefinger on the mahogany panel. He was overreacting.

He had to admit the truth.

It wasn't his appearance, or his age, or his failed marriage that bothered him right now. No, what was bothering him was the upcoming job that King Easton wanted him to do.

For the first time in his life, Harrison wished he wasn't the most trusted adviser and that someone else could fill his role. The upcoming assignment was a job that Harrison knew he would be uncomfortable doing.

Sure, he'd handled worse jobs, dirtier jobs, and even more dangerous jobs. But this job… For once he dreaded duty.

As Harrison stepped off the elevator, Eleanor, King Easton's secretary, stood. "Right on time," she said. "He said to send you straight in as soon as you arrived."

"Thanks, Ellie." The plush carpet muffled the sound of Harrison's Italian shoes.

"You're welcome," Ellie answered in English. A slight accent tinged her voice. Although French was the official language of Korosol, while in America, the royal party spoke fluent English. Ellie nodded toward double doors that marked the entrance to the inner sanctum of the king's American embassy office. A gold Korosolan seal adorned each of the heavy mahogany doors. "Between you and me, he's particularly agitated today."

"I'll take care of it," Harrison said with what he hoped passed for a reassuring smile.

He and Ellie had become good friends from working so closely with the king these past few years, and Harrison knew that underneath her dowdy skirts and her large glasses, Eleanor Standish had the makings of a knockout. It was probably good she hadn't discovered it yet, he mused, or some young man would have snatched the twenty-six-year-old from Easton's service. Right now, with the king's health being questionable, the monarch needed to be Ellie's full focus.

Harrison knocked on the door, the sharp staccato echoing as he waited for Easton's "Enter." Upon hearing it, Harrison walked into the king's sanctum.

"Ah, right on time as usual," Easton said. He glanced up from where he sat behind a large desk. As Harrison approached, Easton put a stack of papers aside.

Harrison executed a bow, one perfected over the years. By now Easton had stopped asking Harrison to perform it. He'd long ago learned that no matter how many times he told Harrison not to bow when they were alone, the younger man would always observe proper etiquette when greeting his king.

"Your Grace," Harrison said. His eyes narrowed as his gaze studied the king. Easton looked a little paler today. Despite his advanced age, Easton still had a full head of gray hair. It may have thinned, but it still made him look younger. Today, however, Easton just looked tired and drawn. He even seemed slightly shrunken, not quite the six feet that still commanded a formidable but wise presence even when seated. Harrison made one more quick assessment of the king's appearance. With the stress he'd been under lately Harrison wasn't too surprised.

Easton hadn't been in New York City for twenty years. That year had been traumatic for Easton. First there had been the failed assassination attempt. Then, following quickly on the heels of that tragedy, King Easton had had to travel to America to bury his youngest son, Drake. He had died when his private plane crashed.

Recently diagnosed with a rare blood condition of unknown origin, King Easton wouldn't be in America now if he didn't desperately need to name an heir to the Korosolan throne.

The trip so far hadn't been successful. Easton's first two choices, Drake's oldest daughters, had both turned down the opportunity to be successor to the crown.

Harrison knew that Easton didn't need any more stress on his already overfull plate.

"Sit down, Harrison." Easton gestured to a chair. "I'm sure you suspect why I've called you here for this meeting."

"I believe I do," Harrison replied as he sat in

the overstuffed leather armchair strategically placed in front of Easton's desk.

He waited for the king to speak. When in private with Harrison, Easton abstained from using what he called his "public speaking persona."

Easton nodded soberly and drew in a long breath before beginning. Then he cut right to the chase. "With CeCe and Amelia now being married, and refusing the crown, that leaves only my granddaughter Lucia."

At Easton's mention of Charlotte Carradigne's youngest daughter, Harrison's gut churned. Only years of practice allowed him to school his face into a neutral mask. He pushed the image of the beautiful blonde out of his mind. He didn't need to think of Lucia. She'd already haunted him enough.

"Lucia is all I have left of Drake's lineage to be queen," Easton stated flatly. "I didn't think it would come to this, but it has. I thought it would be simple, name CeCe and go home. As we know, that didn't happen."

"Yes, Your Grace," Harrison said. Then, because only he could take the liberties afforded to him as the king's right-hand man, he said, "I know how disappointed you are that your plans went awry. But do you think Lucia is suitable?"

Easton sighed before replying, and Harrison saw at once how deeply the whole matter truly had affected his beloved king. "You know me so well,

Harrison. In fact, I wonder if Drake had lived, if he and I would have shared the friendship *we* do.''

Easton's hand shook slightly as he reached slowly for the crystal goblet in front of him. As usual, Ellie had already refilled it with fresh ice water.

Before continuing, Easton took a long drink. ''To answer your question, I don't know about Lucia's suitability. I never would have questioned it, except for the tabloid article.''

''It was quite embarrassing,'' Harrison agreed.

''Exactly. Krissy Katwell is a menace.'' Easton named with distaste the tabloid columnist that kept digging up and exposing the Carradigne family skeletons.

''That woman is dragging the Carradigne name through the proverbial mud,'' the king said. ''This latest mess, interviewing Lucia's ex-fiancé is reprehensible. She quoted him as saying my granddaughter is a fast-and-loose woman.''

Easton's forehead creased and Harrison winced. Easton's stress level had just visibly risen, making his face appear even more drawn. ''Of course,'' Easton continued, ''the tabloid article leaves out the fact that the man was a gold digger only after the family fortune. Have you seen any unacceptable behavior?''

Only my own. Harrison shook his head. ''I saw no inappropriate behavior on Lucia's part at the wedding reception a month or two ago, sir. Even though she brought a rock musician as a date to CeCe's wedding to Shane O'Connell, she displayed nothing but the utmost decorum. She behaved as any princess should.''

Except when she trembled in my arms. Harrison pushed that unsettling thought away. That memory was forbidden, and he didn't need or want to remember that. Lucia Carradigne was strictly off-limits, and should have been that night as well. He should have known better, been more prepared.

Easton didn't seem to sense his friend's momentary discomfort. ''Although at CeCe's reception Lucia behaved properly, I can't risk any more negative press. To my subjects, Krissy Katwell has made Lucia sound like, well, for lack of a better word, a tramp.''

''Surely not,'' Harrison said, meaning the extent of the tabloid's damage to the princess's reputation with the people of Korosol.

Easton misunderstood, thinking Harrison meant the tabloid's damage to Lucia personally. ''Of course Lucia isn't a tramp. That's the furthest thing from the truth. I wish we could sue Katwell for libel, but this is America, not Korosol. What my people must be thinking is beyond me.''

Harrison kept his mouth shut. He knew that Easton knew exactly what was occurring in Korosol, and as usual, that Easton had his fingers firmly on the pulse of his people's views.

Easton straightened up against the back of his leather executive chair. "I need you to investigate Lucia, Harrison. I know I told you to do it earlier, but now it's truly a priority. Time is of the essence. I must be certain that she's fit to be queen of Korosol. I must be sure she doesn't have any other so-called skeletons hiding in her closet, that she's not pregnant, like CeCe was, or already married like Amelia was to Nicholas Standish."

Harrison's facade never changed as he looked at Easton. He'd heard this before, and Easton's repet-itiveness only emphasized the seriousness of the sit-uation. "Yes, sir. This is a wise move on your part, and it's a job I'm qualified to do."

"She's a smart one, my granddaughter Lucia," Easton said with a slight, reminiscing smile. "She reminds me of her father. Headstrong. Independent. Dating the wrong types."

Harrison merely nodded. He'd put off the inevi-table, and now he had no choice. He'd have to be face-to-face with Lucia. Again. Facing her would be worse than facing a bullet, and he knew from actual experience how that felt.

"Harrison—" Easton's voice called Harrison back to the present "—I truly believe that all Lucia needs is to find her true calling, as Drake did when he met Charlotte and fell in love."

A faraway look came over Easton's face. "I had such fears for Drake, but after he met Charlotte they were all for naught. He gave up his inappropriate playboy lifestyle and settled down. He became the perfect father and businessman. Just look at what he did with DeLacey Shipping."

Easton placed his arms across his chest and leaned back farther in his chair. "I feel Lucia will be the same way. All she needs is guidance and direction. Like Drake, she's the youngest child. I've found that the baby of the family often becomes spoiled. Since no one really bothers them much, they often do whatever they want. Maybe it's because by that point parents are too tired from fighting with the older ones, or in this case, one parent died when the children were young. Regardless, my youngest granddaughter has become quite successful in her own right. Her jewelry is lovely, just look at the brooch she gave CeCe and the pendant she gave Amelia."

"They were beautiful," Harrison agreed. Here at least was a neutral topic, one that didn't spark emotions he shouldn't feel. "And she did provide the most exquisite pieces for that woman who just won the Golden Globe for Best Actress. What was her name? Kimberly something?"

"Exactly." Easton nodded. "Lucia has so much undeveloped potential. She moves easily amongst celebrities, the upper crust of society, and even what we'd refer to as the common man. With a little guidance, and if she has no secrets, I believe that she could make a perfect queen for Korosol.''

Harrison nodded his agreement, unnaturally wishing to shorten the meeting. Normally, once their business was concluded, he and Easton would talk on miscellaneous topics, sometimes for hours. ''I will step up the investigation immediately.''

''Good. When I first came to America in February I made it quite clear to the Carradignes that one of them would be my heir. Now it's April and I've wasted enough time. Lucia knows her two sisters were my first choices. Now that they've declined, obviously Lucia knows she's next. So, I've requested her to come to the embassy tomorrow at three.''

''Tomorrow,'' Harrison echoed. He'd see her tomorrow. His mask slipped. ''So soon.''

''Is that a problem?''

Harrison blinked and focused. He'd spoken the words aloud, which was totally uncharacteristic of him. ''Tomorrow is fine.''

''Good. I don't have any more time to waste.''

''Yes, Your Grace,'' Harrison replied. Tomorrow he would see her again. He stiffened. He had a job to do, and he knew he must remember that. Lucia Carradigne was only a job; that was all. Harrison again focused on Easton. Instead of dismissing him,

Easton was still speaking. Harrison tried to pay attention.

"Do yourself one favor," Easton said. "Be honest with Lucia about what you are doing. Tell her you are investigating her. Tell her that if I name her, you will help school her in Korosolan etiquette and customs. Our culture is different from her American upbringing. If I choose her, I don't want her changing her mind. Tell her anything she needs to know to be a suitable queen."

The words came out automatically, although in his mouth they tasted like sandpaper. "I can do that," Harrison replied. *I hope.*

Easton broke into a wide grin, as if for the first time in a while he'd heard good news. "Excellent. Besides, this will be the perfect time for you to get to know Lucia. If my plan works as I desire, I'll get my heir to the throne and you'll have a daughter-in-law."

Harrison felt as if someone had punched him in the solar plexus. Ever since CeCe's wedding over a month ago, it had been apparent to everyone that Easton was playing matchmaker. However, until now, he had never actually voiced the words that he wanted Lucia married to Harrison's son.

Harrison swallowed and somehow managed to answer without revealing how unsettling the thought of Lucia being with Devon was. "Yes, Your Grace."

"Perfect. Report back to me tomorrow on how the first interview went. I want to know everything. Now, call Ellie in here. I'm feeling rather tired, and I believe I'll go back to Charlotte's apartment and rest."

"You are feeling—"

"Fine." Easton abruptly cut off Harrison's statement of concern. "I have a few years left in me, and I refuse to believe that whatever this disease I've contracted is incurable like the doctors maintain. Now, fetch Ellie for me, and I'll speak with you tomorrow."

"Yes, Your Grace." Harrison rose and executed another perfect bow before turning and leaving Easton's office.

Upon seeing Harrison, Ellie rose and immediately went into the office. Harrison stepped into the embassy's private elevators and pushed the button. He was staying in the staff apartments on the fifth floor, and the light glowed ominously, as if sealing his fate.

He'd known this "investigation" was inherent, and for once, he'd put it off. Easton had had to ask twice. Although the monarch didn't seem to mind, Harrison had procrastinated. He never hesitated. He always took the initiative, even finishing tasks early. But not this time.

His reasoning was simple. He couldn't tell Easton everything. He couldn't tell him the truth.

For how could he tell his king, his boss, his friend, that he'd already compromised his position? It had happened over a month ago, the very moment he had first set eyes on Lucia Carradigne at her sister's wedding reception.

CeCe's wedding.

As usual, work had come before pleasure. Thus, Sir Harrison Montcalm had missed all the glitz and glitter of the society event of the season—the wedding of CeCe Carradigne and Shane O'Connell. He hadn't minded. He loved his job.

Therefore, he had been at the embassy checking to see if there were any rumors from Korosol or within the local Korosolan community about Markus's activities. Harrison relished this job. Deep in his gut Harrison never had liked the king's grandson. Harrison's dislike ran so deep that he suspected Markus was responsible for his parents' deaths over a year ago, a suspicion brought to him and Easton by some of Byrum and Sarah's friends who had been on the safari at the same time. It was an awful suspicion to have, but Harrison knew how much Prince Markus wanted the throne. But had the king's grandson stooped to murder? Harrison was determined to find out.

So duty had come before pleasure and Harrison had arrived at the wedding reception after it was already in full swing, long after the dinner plates of the multiple courses had been whisked away. He'd arrived just in time to watch Devon get rid of the very uninvited Krissy Katwell.

And then he'd seen her.

Whoever she was, she was beautiful.

He'd never been partial to blondes, but her dark blond hair perfected her radiant skin tone. The silken strands hung in loose ringlets around her face.

Her smile was wide and wonderful, and just seeing her direct it at someone else had the power to stop Harrison's heart.

Her ball gown's color challenged angels in its brilliance. The striped, form-fitting gown in the Korosolan colors of royal blue and silver only accented her radiance. What little makeup she wore only enhanced her natural beauty.

Even from where he stood on the edge of the dance floor, he could see that her eyes were green. How he could see her eyes from ten feet away was incomprehensible, but somehow Harrison could see, and he just knew.

From afar he basked in her glow, feasting on her beauty like a thirsty man seeing water. For a moment time seemed to stop, and frozen there he knew he'd never felt this way before.

She seemed to sense his scrutiny, for she turned her head and ran her gaze quickly over him. He felt the electric shock from just her look. Then the waltz turned her graceful body away from him.

As the connection broke, Harrison shook himself. Way too young, he told himself simply. Whoever she was, from the way she moved and looked he guessed her to be not more than twenty-six. He had a son older than that.

"Excuse me."

Harrison started as a soft, feminine voice floated over to him. He turned slightly, and there she was. In heels she stood just about eye to eye with his six-foot figure. Up close, her willowy grace was pure beauty, and he blinked just to see if she was truly real or simply the vision of a lonely man.

She touched his sleeve, her fingertips light as feathers. "Would you care to dance?"

Would he? He shouldn't. Excuses rose to his lips. "I…"

"Please," she said softly, her voice a mere silken whisper. "From your uniform I know you're Korosolan, and I would be so grateful. See that man coming this way?" She gestured a manicured finger toward a man headed in their direction. His bright red hair offset his freckles and contrasted with his ill-fitting tuxedo. "That's Larry Zimmer, and no matter how many times I say no, he can't get the picture. Would you perform the duty of helping a lady in distress?"

"I would be honored to," Harrison said. Under

the guise of duty, he took the arm she offered. A frisson of desire shot through him as he guided her to the dance floor.

She linked her hands to his. "Thank you," she said as another waltz began.

Harrison struggled to make light of the moment as he led her around the dance floor. "So you would rather dance with an old man to escape a young one?"

As if she found his comment funny, her smile widened. "What old man? You mean my grandfather? We danced earlier."

Harrison returned her smile with one of his own. "I meant..."

"I know what you meant," she said simply. Her green-eyed gaze held his. "But I figured you needed an excuse. If not, you may never have asked me."

He wouldn't have, either. "You're right," he admitted.

"I know," she replied. "So I helped you along."

Was this woman magic? She'd somehow seen right through him.

"I'm glad you did," he said. And he was. For holding her felt as if he was holding a slice of heaven.

As the music shifted pace, he drew her a little closer. She smelled like roses, and her skin felt like the softest silk. There, during the moments on the

dance floor, Harrison found himself feeling younger, feeling more alive than he'd been in years.

His fingers once grazed the small of her back, and an electric tremor shot through him as her eyes darkened to jade.

"You're a wonderful dancer," she said.

Speak again, Harrison thought, *for to my ears your words are like the purest music.*

"As are you," he replied instead.

She simply acknowledged his return compliment with a slight inclination of her head.

Time never stops for love, Harrison thought as the musical number drew to an end.

"I believe he's gone," he whispered as he guided her off the dance floor.

"He is, but I'd still like to dance with you," she said. "Perhaps this next number?"

"There you are!"

Harrison turned as King Easton came up to him. Being the same height, and after working with the king for such a long time, Harrison wondered why he hadn't noticed the particular color of Easton's eyes before. They reminded him of...

"I see you've met Lucia."

Harrison turned to see whom Easton was referring to.

"Hello again, Grandfather," Lucia replied. She kept her fingers lightly on Harrison's arm. "Are you enjoying the reception?"

"Absolutely," Easton replied. He gestured, and Harrison watched as his son, Devon, came forward. "Here she is, Devon. She was dancing with your father. Now take her out on the dance floor. Lucia's too young to spend her time with all us elderly types."

Harrison grimaced. How old that made him sound!

Lucia gently removed her fingers. "Thank you for the dance," she said politely.

Devon gave her a low bow. "May I have this dance, Princess Lucia?"

"You may, Sir Montcalm," she said as she took his arm.

Harrison watched her go. She glanced back over at him, and then as if remembering her role, she slid into a neutral facade and followed Devon's lead.

"Beautiful, isn't she?" King Easton asked. "While I'm partial to CeCe's beauty because she's so much like my beloved Cassandra," Easton mentioned his deceased wife, "one has to admit that Lucia has an innate beauty that is all her own."

"Indeed," Harrison somehow managed to agree noncommittally. The woman he had been dancing with was Princess Lucia!

"They make such a perfect couple." Easton nodded with a contented smile. "Don't you agree?"

Harrison looked at where his son held Lucia.

She'd bowed her head, and was listening to something he said. A pang of jealousy shot through him. He tamped it down. His duty was, as always, to his king. "They make a good couple," he stated, although his heart wasn't anywhere near the words.

"I think so," Easton said, obviously pleased that Lucia and Devon were beginning their second dance. "Ah, there's Charlotte. Please excuse me, Harrison."

Harrison bowed as the king moved away. Then he turned and took a glass of champagne from a passing waiter. He'd had nothing to drink all evening, for Harrison never drank while in any type of royal capacity, but for tonight he'd make an exception with one glass.

After all, when the woman of your dreams is designated for your son, a little champagne can't hurt.

"Shall we dance again?"

He tensed. He'd know her voice anywhere; already it had imbedded itself into his consciousness and into his soul.

"That wouldn't be proper, Princess Lucia," he replied, his tone deliberately cool.

"Proper?" Lucia frowned. Then a small tight smile came over her face. "Ah, Sir Harrison Montcalm, man of duty, is back in full armor." She saw his surprise. "Your son spent most of his time talking about you, and your many accomplishments."

She lifted a glass of champagne from a waiter and drained it in two gulps.

"Well, Sir Harrison Montcalm, I'm sure someone will fill you in that I'm not always proper. In fact, my date is that rock musician over there. I only brought him because it would annoy my mother, and keep her from playing matchmaker."

With a thump, Lucia placed her empty champagne flute on a nearby table. Harrison winced for the flute.

"While I know all the correct etiquette, I find most of it boring and plain dull," Lucia said.

She stepped toward him, her voice lowered for emphasis. "For some reason I thought you were different. I felt a connection between us, something I can't exactly explain. I wanted to explore it, for whatever it was, I thought it was special."

How her words hurt. Harrison so wanted to tell her that yes, he had felt it too. But duty came first. It always did.

Doing his duty meant he couldn't tell her he'd felt it. He couldn't even be with her. She was a princess.

As much as he wanted to tell her, to explain his reasoning, he kept silent.

For a brief second Lucia looked hurt, and Harrison's stomach churned as her chin rose stubbornly.

"I could order you to dance, couldn't I?" she asked, her gaze never leaving his.

"That you could, Princess."

Lucia nodded, her look now bitterly disappointed. He hated hurting her. "I thought so. Good night, Sir Montcalm."

And with that, she strode off toward her date, a man whose hair was longer than Lucia's.

Harrison set his full flute of champagne down, the bubbly golden liquid untouched. Dancing with her had been a touch of heaven, but Harrison had learned long ago that heaven was not his to have.

He, retired general, Sir Harrison Montcalm, was one, too old for her, and two, not of her social circle. He could not ever have a relationship with a princess, especially the granddaughter of his king, his friend. With a heavy heart, he had turned away.

Chapter Two

The next day Lucia Carradigne was late for her interview.

Harrison paced the plush office allotted him during his stay at Korosol's American embassy. Knowing he'd be seeing her again, he'd dressed even more impeccably than usual for the meeting. He wore a navy blue suit, a tie with the Korosolan crest and a white starched shirt.

Ellie had joked that morning that she'd never seen Harrison looking that put together. He'd run across Markus that morning as well, who since his return from Europe had been lurking around the embassy more than ever. Markus, of course, never missed an opportunity to dig at Harrison. He'd told Harrison he looked like a pallbearer.

Harrison glanced again at his Rolex, a gift from King Easton commemorating twenty-five years of service to the royal family.

Lucia Carradigne was now a half hour late.

A knock sounded at the door, and Harrison turned from where he'd been staring out the window at the United Nations Building.

"Come in," he called.

"Harrison." As Devon entered the room, Harrison's face fell.

"Devon." He greeted his twenty-eight-year-old son easily, although honestly he didn't feel at ease around Devon. After Mary's sudden death from pneumonia, he'd sent the then sixteen-year-old Devon to military school. His son, the serious young man in front of him, was now a man he barely knew.

They couldn't be more apart, despite their similarities. Sure, they both had a military-cut hairstyle. Devon's color was a lighter brown, and was minus the gray that graced Harrison's head. They shared hazel eyes. But they didn't share the closeness of a father and son.

One more of the regrets in his life, Harrison mused with a twinge of bitterness.

If Devon sensed his father's thoughts, he didn't indicate it. Instead, the captain of the Royal Guard and person in charge of Korosol security got right to business.

"I wanted you to know that I'm getting a little closer to where Krissy Katwell may be getting her information. I've been able to secure some of her telephone records," Devon said.

"Legally, of course," Harrison interjected. Inwardly he winced when he saw Devon's expression. Of course his son would do things legally. Devon was a by-the-book type of man.

"Of course," Devon said, quickly covering up his own hurt at being second-guessed by his father.

"Good work," Harrison said, trying to repair his gaffe. "I'm sure you're quite on top of things."

"Yes," Devon replied. He shifted his weight from one foot to the other. "King Easton sent me down here. He said that you were interviewing Princess Lucia and he suggested that it might be to my benefit for security reasons to be present for the interview."

Another matchmaking attempt, Harrison thought with an inward groan. He studied his son thoughtfully for a moment. Devon didn't seem too keen, or too overly eager, to be a part of the interview.

But then, Devon would do what the king wished, no matter what his personal feelings were. Besides, if Devon had personal feelings for the princess, Harrison doubted his son would share them with his father. They'd never been close enough to have ever once shared personal confidences.

"I think I can handle it on my own," Harrison said smoothly. "I believe having to face two Montcalm men might be a bit overwhelming, even for a princess."

"True." Devon nodded. "But King Easton was most insistent."

"I'll explain your absence to the king," Harrison said, sealing his own fate irrevocably. "Right now your time is better spent on discovering where Krissy Katwell is getting her information. You know from our meeting earlier this week about Easton and my suspicions as to her source, and hence, time is of the essence. Krissy Katwell has already done quite a bit of damage to the Carradigne name. She needs to be stopped, and her source silenced."

"Understood." Devon deferred to the judgment of his father, and technically his superior in rank. "I'll report back to you as soon as I know more."

"Very good." Harrison glanced at his watch again. He frowned. Lucia was now forty-five minutes late.

Not a good sign for someone who wanted to be queen. He glanced up at Devon, who was still standing in the office.

Devon had a strange, questioning look on his face as he studied his father. "Harrison, is something wrong?"

It had always bothered Harrison that Devon never called him "Dad" or even "Father." But he didn't dwell on that now. "Princess Lucia was supposed to be here at three."

Devon frowned. As captain of the Royal Guard,

his concern was immediate. "Do you think something has happened to her?"

No. She's making me pay for rejecting her. She's proving who is boss. The insight hit Harrison like a freight train. Being late was the oldest female trick in the book, and here he was, pacing his office and checking his watch every minute.

As quickly as it had come, he dismissed the thought. Lucia didn't strike him as being like that. He contemplated his gut reaction a moment. Instinct told him that Lucia was nothing like Mary. Devon's mother had used those tricks many times. Harrison's instinct was never wrong.

"I think the princess is just running behind," Harrison replied, giving Lucia the benefit of the doubt. "She's a very busy lady, and I'm sure she got caught up in something that was unavoidable."

Devon nodded. "If she doesn't show soon, let me know and I'll find out what's wrong."

"That won't be necessary."

At the silken female voice, both men turned toward the doorway. Harrison sucked in his breath.

Time away from her hadn't diminished his first impressions. As always, she was beautiful. Her dark blond hair fell to her shoulders, and her green eyes darkened as her gaze found Harrison.

"Hello, Harrison," she said.

Belatedly, Harrison remembered he needed to

bow. He and Devon both scrambled and bowed low.

"Princess Lucia." Harrison tried to maintain a formal tone as he straightened. "Please come in. It's good to see you." He reached for the coat she was shedding.

She gave him a genuine smile as her fingers lightly touched his while transferring the garment. "It's good to see you too, Harrison. I trust I'm finding you well?"

"Of course," he said, realizing too late that somehow she'd already gained the upper hand by again calling him by his first name.

"Are you going to be present for this interview, Sir Devon?" As Lucia turned and faced the younger man, Harrison took a moment to study what Lucia wore. He'd heard she usually wore bohemian-type clothing, like flowing skirts and peasant blouses. But today was different. Like at the wedding reception, she appeared regal, refined. Her pale pink trouser suit celebrated the start of spring. The color suited her.

"No, Princess. I was just leaving. If you'd please excuse me." Devon bowed again and posted a hasty retreat.

Lucia turned and faced Harrison. He managed to swallow, and somehow years of training kept his face immobile. That was until she turned on the charm and smiled widely again the moment they were alone. "Yes, I must say that it's good to see you, Harrison. I've been looking forward to this interview ever since my grandfather called me and told me about it."

Harrison somehow managed an appropriate gesture to a seat. As Lucia sat down, her perfume wafted past him. She smelled like roses again.

She looked expectantly at him. "So if you're ready?"

Inwardly Harrison groaned. Where Lucia was concerned, he doubted he would ever be ready.

SHE HADN'T MEANT to be late. But someone had slipped down onto the subway tracks, delaying the trains uptown for a good half hour.

Lucia settled herself into the chair as Harrison brought her a glass of ice water. Perhaps she should have taken a taxicab as her mother always insisted. After all, as the past two months had demonstrated, she was a princess, and therefore she could technically be a target of a kidnapping attempt. But still Lucia valued her anonymity too much to give it up yet.

She thrived in New York City's sea of anonymous faces. A people-watcher by nature, Lucia credited a lot of her creative genius to just watching the interactions of the everyday world. The panhandler holding the cup in Times Square had inspired a collection of dimpled platinum pins. The mother nursing her child on a Central Park bench had inspired a series of interlocking linked gold bracelets with birthstones.

Even today, the successful rescue mission had been, in a sense, inspirational. New Yorkers working together—Lucia could already visualize the brooches of intertwined pieces of silver and gold metal.

If only she and Harrison could work together. Couldn't he feel the frisson of electricity that passed through their fingertips every time they touched, like now as he handed her the water?

"Thank you," she said.

"You're welcome," Harrison replied. As he sat down across from her, she took a minute to sip her water and study him.

What was it about this man? Ever since she'd first set eyes on him, from across the dance floor, everything about him had impressed her.

She'd never been partial to short, military-style haircuts, but on Harrison, she couldn't imagine any other thing. She'd never even thought she'd be attracted to a military man. They were too by the book, too punctual, too precise. But, with what little she'd learned of Harrison since the wedding reception, she couldn't imagine him any other way.

"I've rescheduled my four-o'clock appointment so we have all the time necessary," Harrison told her.

"Oh, I'm sorry," Lucia began. Then she stopped. She was a princess. Of course he would reschedule for her. But she didn't like the idea that he thought she'd deliberately been late. Perhaps she should tell him about the subway. She sipped her water and contemplated it for a moment. No, just like her mother, he'd probably disapprove of her public-transport choices. She kept silent.

"I must ask your pardon for the nature of the questions that I'm going to have to ask, Princess," Harrison said. "Some of them may be personal. You, of course, do not need to answer any that you do not wish to. This is not an interrogation."

"Yes, my grandfather explained it to me." Lucia nodded. "He wants to determine my suitability. After my sisters, I don't blame him."

Harrison arched his eyebrows. "You don't? Excuse me, I shouldn't have asked that."

"You can ask what you wish," Lucia said. "And of course, I do not blame my grandfather, especially after what's happened." Lucia shook her head vigorously, which caused her hair to fall in her face. She brushed the blond strands back. "CeCe was pregnant, and Amelia already secretly married. I just hope I don't disappoint him as well. Whereas my grandfather and I have not seen each other in years, I do care for him a great deal."

"Well." Harrison coughed. "Your suitability is what we'll try to determine. First, if King Easton does declare you his heir, I must know if you are willing to accept the full role and all it entails. Are you willing to be the queen of Korosol?''

Was she? For a moment Lucia thought of her mother. Now that Charlotte had warmed to the idea of one of her daughters being queen, Charlotte had become like a dog with a meaty bone. Lucia knew that, in her mother's eyes, she was it. Charlotte had been on Lucia's case for days, warning her not to mess this opportunity up.

Maybe for once she wouldn't disappoint her mother in something. Whereas her mother might wish Lucia queen, Lucia herself still had doubts. ''I am quite prepared to fulfill the role if King Easton chooses me,'' Lucia said, proud she managed to deliver the words without a betraying quiver in her voice.

''Then we begin,'' Harrison said.

Lucia simply nodded, and for one childish moment wished she had someone there to hold her hand.

''Again, Princess, I ask your pardon in the nature of these questions, but I must ask you about your ex-fiancé Gregory Barrett and the allegations he made in Krissy Katwell's column.''

''That what, I'm a fast-and-loose woman? In his dreams.'' Hackles rose on Lucia's spine. Realizing what her outburst must have sounded like, she covered her mouth with her fingers. ''Sorry, that's not very princesslike, but whenever I think of him, well..." She shuddered with revulsion.

"Why don't you tell me about him?"

"The man is a liar and a cheat." Lucia leaned forward, suddenly desperate to have Harrison's approval. "I was twenty-three when we met at some art gallery premiere one of my mother's favorite charities was hosting. I'm not sure what the cause was."

"That doesn't matter," Harrison said. He reached forward and took a Cross pen and leather portfolio off an occasional table. "Please continue."

She watched his fingers and thumb roll the pen between them. "You're going to take notes?"

Harrison looked up, and Lucia saw the surprise he quickly masked, as if his reach for the items had been more of a protective device—a need to occupy his hands as if to calm nerves. "If you don't mind. King Easton wants a full report."

Lucia thought for a moment. Did she make him nervous? She'd have to contemplate that more at a later time. "No, I don't mind." She bit her lower lip, and then she remembered that her mother had scolded her out of that habit long ago. She set her lip free. "Gregory seemed to be just the type a girl could bring home to Mother, and actually, I guess that's what I found attractive about him. Mother and I don't necessarily have the best relationship."

She turned to Harrison. "How does that happen?"

"What?" Harrison asked. He stopped writing, and his hazel gaze connected with Lucia's.

"Well, two people are related by blood yet they seem to have absolutely nothing in common. I mean, look at you and Devon. He's following in your footsteps and obviously worships you. I'm just trouble with a capital T to my mother."

Harrison set the pen down. "I doubt your mother thinks that."

"Oh, she does." Lucia nodded, her hair falling in her face again. "When I chose not to go into the shipping business, I heard how much of a disappointment I was to her. I mean, she's devoted all her life to the family company and building it. She's the head of it, and it's more her baby than I am. She was not happy with my choice."

"Parents sometimes say things that they don't mean," Harrison said.

"It doesn't matter. You wouldn't understand. Devon is such a success and a credit to you."

"I'm far from the ideal father." The admission spilled from Harrison's mouth before he could stop it.

Lucia raised an eyebrow in disbelief. "I can't believe that."

"Believe it." The cat already out of the bag, Harrison cocked his head and gave Lucia a wry smile. "I failed not only my wife but my son as well. If I'd been any type of good father I would have known what to do with my son when his mother died. Instead, I shipped him off at age sixteen to the military academy. So don't judge your mother so harshly. Perhaps she only thought she was doing what was best."

Lucia smiled and the movement lit up her whole face. "You know, you may be right," Lucia said finally. "My mother did work very hard to keep the shipping business going so that we could be raised in the proper environment befitting what my father would have wished. I just wish that included letting us visit Korosol, though. Since my father's death she's sworn off going again and so I don't remember anything about it. I was too young."

"It's lovely there," Harrison told her honestly.

"Tell me about it," she said.

"I've never seen water so clear, grass so green or flowers so yellow," Harrison said. "Part of the country is the Larella Mountains, and part is on the Mediterranean coast. There the beaches are the whitest and softest sand."

"I've seen pictures," Lucia said, "and it looks lovely. Once I even ordered the tourist brochures on the village of Aladair. I never did get to visit, though."

Harrison smiled at her. "I've traveled the world, and to me, it will always be home. I can't imagine living any other place. I guess I get my energy from the land.''

Lucia nodded. ''Like Scarlett O'Hara.''

''Who?''

''The heroine in *Gone With the Wind*. She got her strength from the red earth of her plantation, Tara. You mean you've never seen the movie? It's one of my all-time favorites.''

''Uh, no,'' Harrison admitted. With his military career, he hadn't had time to see many movies, even on video.

''We'll have to watch it.'' Lucia's face grew animated and, despite himself, knowing he shouldn't, Harrison delighted in watching her.

''I love classic movies,'' Lucia said, ''and this one won ten Academy Awards, including 1939 Best Picture. I can't believe you haven't seen it.''

''Well, believe it,'' Harrison said with a smile.

''Then at one of these interviews we'll watch *Gone With the Wind* so you'll really know what I'm referring to.''

''Speaking of the interview, perhaps we should get back to our subject.''

At Harrison's statement, Lucia's euphoria fell, but she didn't let him see. ''Yes, we probably should.''

She masked her disappointment with a smile of acceptance. He'd actually talked to her—amazing.

For a brief moment she'd seen him loosen up, seen him out of the role that he was so entrenched in.

Yes, she'd been right that night of the wedding reception. Harrison Montcalm was a man who was in desperate need of a little freedom from the restrictions he'd placed on his own life.

And if her mother wanted Lucia to find a proper man, Harrison was as proper as they came.

Briefly, as she watched him study his notepad, Lucia contemplated the fact that Harrison was nineteen years older than herself. She watched as his firm fingers used the pen to jot a note on the pad. She shivered slightly. Age didn't matter. In her acquaintances with artists, musicians and people of "improper" society, according to her mother, Lucia had learned that appearances didn't matter. It was what was inside the person that was truly important.

She wanted to know what was inside Harrison Montcalm. If her suspicious were right, and they always were, deep inside Harrison was a heart of gold.

Harrison looked up and caught her staring at him. Her cheeks flamed pink. "You were telling me about Gregory Barrett," he said.

"Oh, right," Lucia replied. She didn't want to talk about Gregory. Instead, she wanted to learn about Harrison. "To make a long story short, I dated him and he literally swept me off my feet. We were engaged after two months, and we'd set a wedding date. It was when the Carradigne family lawyers insisted on a prenuptial agreement that things began to fall apart.'' She paused. Then Greg's true colors had become quite obvious.

"As for me being fast and loose, that was Greg and his mouth. He used my relationships with my friends against me. He insinuated that every male friend I had was a boyfriend so that he could make himself look like such a victim. According to him, I used him, chewed him up and spit him out. In reality, he didn't love me. He just wanted a piece of the Carradigne pie. When the lawyers showed him how little he'd get, he said I'd cheated on him. He called me unfaithful so he could dump me like a hot potato and go after some other gullible girl with a trust fund he could pilfer.''

Harrison didn't look up from the leather portfolio, although Lucia could tell he wasn't writing anything. "He worked on Wall Street?''

"Had. Bad investments got him in trouble and fired. So he needed my cash, and fast.'' Lucia shuddered. Gregory's deception had made her leery of men, especially ones that Charlotte found for her. "Do you want to know if we slept together?''

Harrison's head snapped up, and to Lucia's surprise he physically recoiled at that announcement. "That's not necessary.''

Lucia jutted her chin forward. To her, making

Harrison understand was necessary. "Well, we didn't. Have sex, that is."

Harrison straightened. He seemed uncomfortable. "Princess Lucia, King Easton is not concerned about your, um, morality in your choice of, uh, companions. As long as you have been discreet before you take the throne, and as long as, once you become queen, you remain chaste in the eyes of the public until you marry, he will be satisfied that he has made a wise choice."

"What about you?" Lucia turned the question around. "Do you think he's made a wise choice?"

She had to give him credit. He was quick and diplomatic. "It is not my place to judge, Princess. I am just to gather the facts, and if the king chooses you, then I will be your adviser and prepare you for your transition to the throne."

"But you have judged me," Lucia replied, going back to her real question. He had avoided it, and somehow she knew he had judged her. She felt it deep in her bones, and her female intuition never failed her.

"No, Princess, I have not," Harrison denied. "That is not my role as an adviser to the king."

"So you just do what Easton tells you," Lucia returned, her tone a bit harsh.

Harrison blinked, as if surprised by her sudden change of attitude. "I do not understand what you are insinuating, Princess. I do my job."

For one second Lucia wondered why it mattered to her, why she was pursuing this line of conversation. But she knew. It was because of sleepless nights he'd caused her. Because of the erotic dreams she'd had. Because of the feeling of loneliness that had vanished when she'd touched him at the wedding reception. Because of a desire...

She brushed those thoughts aside. She would make him see. "Your job. Do you ever think of more than your job?"

"I think of my duty to the throne."

She wasn't reaching him. "What about passion? What about love?"

Harrison's chin came forward, indicating his stubbornness. "My duty comes first."

"So you've shut off those emotions," Lucia challenged. She wondered why she suddenly felt so determined, so forceful in her questioning. She mentally cursed herself. She knew why.

"Those emotions have no place in rational judgments," he said.

"So passion and love are bad things."

"Passion can get people pregnant at seventeen," Harrison retorted. "Love does not last, and can compromise duty."

"Which you know from personal experience."

"As a matter of fact, I do. It is not one of the better moments in my life."

Lucia nodded, satisfied. Now she was getting somewhere. She'd been right. Harrison Montcalm had buried the passion and fire that still existed in him. Someone—she—just had to dig deep to free it and get it out.

"You don't mind, Harrison, if I question you. After all, if I'm named queen, you've told me you will be my adviser."

"I would," Harrison answered stoically.

"Ah yes, because it would be your duty." Lucia reached forward and refilled her water glass from the crystal pitcher sitting on the table. "Do you ever think of yourself first?"

"No." The pen made a clicking sound as Harrison set it on the table.

"Why not?"

"Because my duty is to serve others," he replied. "Look, excuse me, Princess, but we are getting off track here."

"Call me Lucia, please, Harrison."

"It's not proper."

"I don't care." Lucia smiled, giving him another infuriating smile that she knew was driving Harrison crazy. "My name is Lucia and when we are alone I want you to use it. Consider it an order if that will make your sense of duty feel better."

"Yes, Prin— Lucia."

"Thank you." Lucia nodded her head. "Being friends will help this process go so much smoother, Harrison."

"Our role doesn't involve friendship, Princess."

"Lucia."

"Lucia." His tone indicated his frustration with the entire situation.

She nodded her approval at his use of her name. "You may not like it, Harrison, but you and I should be friends. When I move to Korosol I'll be leaving everything behind. All my friends, my family, everything I've held dear my entire twenty-six years. You'll be one of the only people I'll know. Therefore, we need to be friends."

"That does sound logical," Harrison conceded, and Lucia smiled. She was wearing him down. If nothing else, she was tenacious. She'd finally won her freedom from her mother—the freedom to live her life away from DeLacey Shipping. If she could do that, she could do anything—including making Harrison see things her way.

"Good." She paused as an idea took hold. "You understand that this means we need to get to know each other as friends. Besides, it will fit in with your investigation as to my suitability for the throne. So, since you want to find out the truth about me, I suggest you spend the weekend with me and judge me for yourself."

"It is not my role to judge," he returned to that argument.

Lucia took a sip of water. "Ah, but you must make a report to my grandfather. Thus, if you want to really know everything there is to know about me, you need to spend time with me."

"I don't believe that this is necessarily a good idea."

"Why not?"

As Lucia threw the challenge back into his face,

Harrison asked himself the same question. Why not? The answer was simple. Lucia Carradigne was as off-limits as a nuclear reactor. Despite his attraction to her, today he'd managed to control himself and handle himself with the utmost decorum. For his own sanity and security, he needed to stay away from her.

Already he'd slipped up. Just by being with her he had somewhere along the line lost control of the interview. But it had a positive result. Because of it, he'd seen the real Lucia. And he liked her. A lot.

Lucia. He said her name mentally, rolling it silently over his tongue. He could imagine calling her by her name during lovemaking.

He shook his head, clearing it of that off-limits mental picture. Lucia may be a touch of heaven, but his job did not include holding it, or touching it, or tasting it. Just because she was the first woman to make him feel alive in years, that didn't mean he had to act on it. He'd made a career of doing the right thing, acting the correct way. As soon as King Easton was satisfied with her credentials, Lucia Carradigne would be heir to the Korosol throne.

Retired generals didn't marry princesses, or much less even become their friends. It just wasn't done. Especially not retired generals his age with his baggage.

"Well?" Lucia's voice cut through his disturbing thoughts. "I assume you're deciding if you're going to hang out with me this weekend?"

Hang out? Harrison hadn't heard that word used

in his military circle in years. With free time a premium, he never simply "hung out." Inwardly he groaned. Lucia's words showed how young she really was, but also how much the idea of simply "hanging out" with her appealed to him.

But he couldn't let her know.

"I see that I have little choice in the matter," he replied.

Lucia gave him a seductive smile. "We always have choices, Harrison. I'd just like to think that you made the correct one."

"Time will tell." He managed not to let her know just how much her smile, and her words, had affected him.

"Yes, it will," she said. She glanced at her watch. How time had flown! "Speaking of the time, I didn't realize how late it is. I'm meeting my mother and King Easton for dinner. I need to leave or I'll be late for that, too."

Lucia rose to her feet. "May I please have a piece of your paper?"

Harrison stood, removed his notes and handed her the leather folder and the Cross pen. Lucia took it and wrote quickly.

"Here are the directions. Meet me there at ten. Casual attire." She looked over his business suit. "Definitely not what you have on."

Harrison's eyebrows shot up.

"Not that there's anything wrong with your suit," Lucia reassured him quickly. "You look, well, very nice," she finished awkwardly.

He looked fabulous, debonair and extremely handsome, but she wasn't about to tell him that. Although she was usually very forward and proud of it, something about Harrison made her slightly shy. His opinion mattered, and today she'd already been forward enough. She blinked, trying not to contain her excitement at the prospect of a "date" with Harrison.

"Anyway," she said, "there will probably be a line of people outside the club, so just walk by it and give your name at the door."

Lucia pressed the piece of paper into his hand. "Until tonight at ten."

And then, before he had a chance to bow, Lucia left the office.

HARRISON STARED after her. The proof was all there—the piece of paper crumbled in his palm, the empty water goblet, the residual smell of roses. She hadn't been a mirage.

Why did he feel she had been?

Without her, the room seemed empty, lifeless.

Harrison slumped back down into the chair. He ran a hand thoughtfully across his chin, feeling the five-o'clock shadow that he'd need to shave away before he met up with Lucia tonight.

He couldn't let himself look forward to the evening. But how he wanted to!

Somehow Lucia had triggered something in him, something he needed to explore. He could control it, whatever it was. After the incident with Mary, he'd made being in control a lifelong habit.

The phone on the desk buzzed and Harrison strode over to pick it up.

"King Easton would like to see you before he returns to Charlotte's apartment," Ellie told him. "He informs me he's dining with Lucia and her mother tonight, and he'd like to know if you've discovered anything."

Great. Easton wanted a full report already. Harrison wished he had something to say, besides Lucia's side of Gregory Barrett's story.

For right now, though, that would have to be enough.

"I'll be right up," he said, knowing that once again he was going to lie to his king. But what else could he do?

Torn, he headed toward the elevator, already rehearsing his lines.

Chapter Three

Prince Markus Carradigne was standing in the embassy's huge atrium lobby when the elevator doors opened.

"Lucia!"

She stepped out, her surprise evident. "Markus!" She accepted the kiss her thirty-five-year-old cousin gave her on the cheek.

"What are you doing here?" Markus said pleasantly. "I'm here all the time, but I don't think I've ever remembered you stepping foot in the embassy before."

"Actually, I don't think I ever have been here," Lucia replied. She thought for a moment. "Maybe I came here once with my father when I was a very young child, but I don't remember. So probably not."

"Well, you are looking lovely. A breath of fresh air in this stuffy old place," he said.

Lucia laughed. She'd always been fond of Markus, although lately she'd been wary of him. He'd always made no secret of his desire for the throne of Korosol, and his obsession with it—especially now that Easton was here—was almost creepy.

Still, Markus had been nothing but nice to her and he was charming. Of course, it was too bad his hairline was beginning to recede a little and his gut was starting to expand. If Harrison could keep fit, why couldn't Markus?

The little white lie coming from her mouth slid out with ease. "What is it with people thinking everything is old lately? You look younger every time I see you. It must be that new girlfriend of yours."

"Ah, if you weren't my cousin, Lucia, I'd be the first in line to snatch you up," Markus said with a laugh. "You are such a flatterer. Seriously, though, what brought you by?"

Lucia shrugged. "I had an appointment."

Markus nodded, his blue eyes speculative. "Did it concern what I've been reading in the paper lately? Have Krissy Katwell's columns shaken the king up a bit?"

"Perhaps. But you, probably better than anyone, know our grandfather. I know we all thought his choice for an heir would have been you."

For a moment a dark shadow crossed over Markus's face. Then it flickered away as if it hadn't been there at all. "Yes, well, it's his prerogative to name a successor," he said with a slight laugh.

"That's the Korosolan law. Perhaps he's just making sure he has left no stone unturned or something like that."

"Perhaps he thinks it's too soon after the death of your parents for you to deal with all the pressures of ruling." Lucia placed a hand on Markus's arm. "I'm still so sorry about your parents, Markus. Even after a year, it must be difficult for you."

"Yes, it is," Markus replied. He lifted his arm and adjusted his silk tie.

"Well, it was good seeing you. I've got to get going. I'm already late and you know how my mother is. She's probably chomping at the bit that I'm not doing what's proper."

"You just stay true to yourself, cousin."

"Oh, I try, Markus. I try." Lucia accepted another kiss on the cheek. "Take care." With that she moved through the revolving doors and out onto the sidewalk where she had the security guard hail her a cab.

Markus watched her depart and then turned as his right-hand man, Winston Rademacher, appeared at his side. "So, did your accidental encounter with Lucia confirm what we suspected?" Winston asked. His dark brown eyes were even squintier than normal as they gazed at where Lucia had been standing just moments before.

"Yes," Markus replied. A bitterness filled him.

"She had an appointment with the king. She's obviously Easton's next choice."

"Really?" Winston rolled the word nastily off his tongue. "How very interesting."

"Yes, it is," Markus replied. The lobby was empty, although anyone overhearing the conversation would never understand the undercurrents buzzing between the two men. To anyone observing, the conversation was totally innocent.

Markus clenched his fist and shoved it in his pants pocket. "It seems as if Easton has settled on the youngest daughter now."

"I'll check into it," Winston said.

Markus simply nodded. "See that you do."

LUCIA HAD BARELY arrived at her mother's apartment before Charlotte went on the attack. "So how did it go?" her mother asked.

"Fine," Lucia said. She shrugged and handed Quincy, the family butler, her coat. "Sir Montcalm asked me questions and I answered them."

"Devon?" Her mother looked excited at that prospect.

"No, Harrison," Lucia replied.

"Oh, the older one," Charlotte said dismissively.

"He's younger than you," Lucia said. Her mother gasped and inwardly Lucia winced. That had been cruel. "Sorry," she mumbled as she entered the Grand Room.

Right now she'd rather be talking to Hester Vanderling, Quincy's wife. Because Charlotte had been working, Hester had been Lucia's nanny. Lucia considered Hester more of her confidante than Charlotte.

"So you didn't see Devon?"

"Only for a moment," Lucia said. She poured herself a tall glass of ice water. "I'm sure he has more important work to do than to sit around. Harrison handled the interview fine."

Charlotte twisted the triple strand of freshwater pearls she wore around her neck. They had been an anniversary gift from Drake. She always wore the pearls, especially when she wore one of her designer suits. Today's was baby blue, accenting her blue eyes and white hair. "Easton said he was going to have Devon sit in on the interview," Charlotte said.

Lucia rolled her eyes. "He didn't. Look, Mum, could you just stop playing matchmaker for once?"

A stricken look crossed Charlotte's face. "You know I only want what's best for you. Sir Devon is such a good man and so handsome."

Not as handsome as his father, Lucia thought. She sipped her water. Plus, when she'd danced with Devon at CeCe's reception, he hadn't made her knees feel wobbly the way Harrison had.

"Besides," Charlotte said, "as queen you probably need a prince consort. Who better than Sir

Devon? He's your age, and he knows everything about Korosol. Together you could outshine Princess Diana and Prince Charles in their heyday.''

"Look how that turned out," Lucia pointed out. "I'll marry for love, and I prefer to find it myself."

The arrival of King Easton saved her from having to discuss the matter further.

Dinner was a quiet affair, and after being told all of Sir Devon's merits, Lucia longed to steal off into the kitchen and talk to Hester. Finally, after Charlotte and Easton retired to Charlotte's study to discuss a business problem of Charlotte's, Lucia found her chance.

"Ah, wondered when you'd steal way," Hester said. She accepted the warm kiss Lucia pressed onto the skin of her sixty-something cheek.

"I had to listen to the sale's pitch of why I should marry Sir Devon Montcalm first," Lucia said.

Hester nodded. "Heard them rehearsing it just the other night."

"Well, I wish they'd stop."

"Found someone yourself, have you?" Hester placed the last dish in the dishwasher and turned it on. "Come tell me about him."

"He's perfect," Lucia said. "Handsome, debonair, polite. He's everything any mother could want for her daughter."

Hester and Lucia took seats at the kitchen table.

"So what's the problem? Why haven't you dangled him under your mother's nose?"

"A relationship with me could cost him his job. His age would make it too improper—although I am totally fine with it," Lucia said slowly. She'd been mulling over her predicament with Harrison on the way here. "I think he wants me, but his sense of duty is too great to let himself think that he could love me."

Hester made a tsking sound. "That doesn't sound good, but it's not insurmountable. Look at Quincy. It took him a while to woo me. You're a modern girl. In this day and age, you can woo him."

"But his job," Lucia said. "It means everything to him."

"Nah," Hester said. "He only thinks it does. Men are like that. Dogs with bones they are. Can't see the Meaty Choice in the bowl in front of them."

"I wish it were that simple," Lucia said. "But, like I said before, there's a slight problem with his age."

"Are you robbing the cradle? Shame on you," Hester teased to lighten Lucia's mood.

Lucia wrapped a strand of hair around her finger. She could tell Hester, but still, saying the words was hard. "I'm not, but some might say he is."

Hester's eyes widened. "He's older than you."

"Much," Lucia confirmed. "He has a son who is older than me."

"Ooh," Hester said. "Your mother won't like that."

"My grandfather won't like it either," Lucia said. "It's Harrison."

Hester's fingers flew up to cover her open mouth. "Oh, child. Do you know what you're doing?"

"More than I did with Gregory Barrett," Lucia said. "He makes me feel as if I'm the only one in the world. I don't care about his age. I care about him."

Hester shook her head. "You're in love with him."

"Yes. No. I mean, how could I be?" Lucia wrung her hands.

"Love's like that," Hester said with a sage nod. "It chooses you, and when it hits, you can't escape. It's the most wonderful and frightening feeling in the world."

"I could cost him everything."

"If he loves you, he'll find it worth the cost."

"I can't do that, Hester. He can't ever know how I feel. He can only know that I want him, but not why. He can't know that I could love him, only that I lust for him."

"I don't like it," Hester said. "You've got to be honest with him."

"I can't," Lucia said. "I have to play this right, or I'll lose it all. He'll lose it all. Besides, we only have such a short time to be together. Surely you can see that.''

''When will you see him next?''

''Tonight.''

Hester put her arms around Lucia. ''I hope you know what you're doing.''

Lucia accepted Hester's hug. Being in her nanny's arms had always been the greatest comfort. ''I don't. I'm making it up as I go along. Just be here for me.''

''I always am,'' Hester reassured her. ''I always am.''

As THE CAB approached the club, the music from inside blared so loudly that Harrison could hear it from a block away.

''Dey be jammin' in dat joint,'' the Jamaican cabbie told him as the cab pulled to the curb. The line stretched all the way down the street. ''Hottest spot in da city right now. Fare be twenty-two bucks.''

Harrison handed the man thirty.

''Dank you.'' The cabbie's gold tooth glistened. ''Have fun, and here be my card. Call me to pick you up.''

''Thanks.'' Harrison pocketed the worn business card as he stepped out onto the curb. Despite the chill in the air, a line of strangely dressed people snaked along the curb.

Harrison glanced at his overcoat. Underneath he wore a pair of black wool trousers and a casual black shirt. Most of the crowd waiting on the pavement appeared to be in some form of leather.

His idea of casual and Lucia's were obviously different.

As instructed, he strode past the line and descended down the steps. At the bottom of the stairwell a man with purple hair gave him a curious look.

"Harrison Montcalm," Harrison said, by now feeling completely like a fish out of water. "I'm on the list."

"Ah, Lucia's guest." The man nodded as if that explained everything. He didn't even check a list. "I just need to stamp your hand. She's already paid your cover." The beefy man put a triangular stamp on Harrison's left hand. Harrison looked at it with revulsion. "Go on in and take the freight elevator up to the third floor. She'll be there."

The man clicked a counter, and within a moment Harrison found himself on a freight elevator with another man, this one with a multitude of piercings covering his ears, nose and eyebrows. The man lifted the wooden slats when the elevator stopped at the third floor, and within two seconds Harrison found himself in a world he hadn't seen for over twenty years.

Disco lights flickered and flared, although the

music thumping was anything but disco. People gyrated everywhere, some drinking long-neck bottles of beer, some drinking some sort of fruity concoctions in oversize fishbowls. Spiked hair raged everywhere, and leather outfits that showed everything seemed the standard dress on all the women.

Harrison took off his overcoat and deposited it with the girl—yes, she was a girl; the Mohawk threw him—working the coat check. She gave him an odd look, but said nothing about his attire.

But why should she? This club, in the area of the city called SoHo, for south of Houston Street, seemed to accept everyone.

"Don't call it Houston," the cabbie had told Harrison during the journey. "It's 'How stun.'"

With his coat secured, Harrison moved deeper into the club. Here, in a large open room of at least two stories in height people grooved on the dance floor. Others jived to the beat on the balconies surrounding the center area. Harrison turned his gaze toward the stage.

For a moment he frowned, a sense of déjà vu filling him. The longhaired man playing the lead guitar as if his life depended on it looked familiar.

"Isn't Charles great?" some woman with bright orange hair next to him yelled. She was tossing promotional CDs into the air as she spoke. "This band will be the next big thing. Mark my words. God, I wish my label had signed them first."

Harrison watched her toss more CDs in the air. Even while dancing, people still managed somehow to grab the freebies. Harrison shook his head. Just how long had he been out of the music-club scene? He didn't want to contemplate it. Official state functions and society events like CeCe's wedding still used big bands or quartets that specialized in classical music.

It had been forever since he'd experienced the driving, life-force rock'n'roll now pounding through his veins like a freight train. The lead singer was singing something about "My Madonna," and how he "can't believe she's mine."

And then he saw her.

MOVING IN TIME with the music, Lucia rhythmically weaved her way through the dancers.

Expertly she dodged someone slinging a drink, and then she moved past two people needing to get a room before they carried on any further.

"Harrison." As if she was the only one in the room, somehow he heard her through the din of music as she slid up next to him and put her fingers lightly on his sleeve. "I'm glad you came." She smiled, deciding to tease him just a little. "You're even on time."

"You're early," he said, and then mentally cursed himself for that inane comment. Never had he felt so tongue-tied. Was this the woman, the same woman in the ball gown and the same woman in the pink suit? It had to be, yet, in essence, it wasn't.

Unlike her previous outfits, which had covered her legs, tonight Lucia wore a black miniskirt. Harrison swallowed. With a skirt that came to just mid-thigh, her black hose-clad legs seemed to go on and on forever. The shirt she wore was a white-and-black polka-dot top with oversize sleeves and ruffled cuffs. Two discreet ruffles crisscrossed, and the whole shirt wrapped and knotted at her waist.

Lucia wore her hair crimped, as if she'd curled all the blond locks with a hot iron and run her fingers through her hair to create an effect that was, in a word, breathtaking. Harrison couldn't remove his gaze from her. Unlike many of the clubgoers, Lucia's makeup remained discreet. Only her lipstick, a bright red, was a concession to the atmosphere. On Lucia, though, the result wasn't tawdry or brassy. To him she still remained refined, elegant and lovely.

Her green eyes shone as if they were emeralds, and Harrison found the words slipping out of his mouth before he could even think to stop them. "You look lovely, Lucia."

A slow, sensual smile spread across her face. "Thank you," she replied simply. "I'm thrilled you came. I had my doubts that you'd make it."

"You ordered me to," he reminded her.

"Sort of," she said, her smile never wavering. "But my wanting you here tonight has nothing to do with your duty to Korosol."

She saw his look of surprise and laughed lightly. "Despite what you said last time, I decided that I did want one more dance with you, and no matter how much you pretended otherwise, I know you wanted it, too."

Her admission and assertion floored him. Harrison simply stared, seeing the honesty written all over her face. Lucia wasn't playing games; she was dead serious.

Harrison swallowed again. While he hadn't been perfectly celibate after Mary's death, his encounters had been few and far between. And, while some women would proposition him with the bold audacity of Lucia Carradigne, none of those women ever had affected him as Lucia was doing right now.

He wavered, desperate for the control that for some reason he felt he was losing, if he hadn't already lost it altogether.

Harrison was a man never out of control.

Until now. Until Lucia.

"I'm not really dressed for this place," he told her flatly.

She tightened her grip on his arm and stared intently into his hazel eyes. "You are perfect. Besides, no matter what you wear, I will always be honored to be with you.''

Harrison believed her. The truth of it was right there in those emerald eyes, eyes that looked at him not as a princess or a daughter would, but rather as a lover would.

He began to step aside, to move out of her magnetic proximity, a proximity that threatened every ounce of control and duty he had. Her hand on his arm stopped him. ''What would you like to drink?''

''I don't drink while on duty,'' he told her.

''Water then,'' she said without missing a beat or correcting his assertion that he was ''on duty.'' ''Come. There are people I want you to meet, and of course we must dance.''

''Lucia, really I don't think this is...''

As she paused for a moment to let some people pass, she looked back over her shoulder at him. She turned suddenly and put a hand lightly on his cheek. ''Don't think, Harrison. Feel. For tonight, promise me you'll feel. Feel the music. Feel the night. Feel the magic.''

''I can't do that,'' he told her honestly, for in essence, Harrison really had no idea how to feel. Feelings were dangerous to military men. Thinking, logic, that was what won wars, what kept kingdoms standing. He'd long ago shut down that part of him that knew how to feel, how to experience true emotion.

Lucia smiled and stroked her hand down his cheek. Her fingers warmed his skin, and he felt a sudden chill when she lifted her hand away. Immediately he wanted her hand back on his face. It was like a balm to his soul.

"You can, and you will," she said simply, referring to his belief that he couldn't feel. Her right hand gripped his, and with her left she gestured him to follow her.

As she led Harrison through the crowd, Lucia tried to concentrate on the job at hand.

Hand. A thrill shot through her. The job at hand literally had his hand in hers. Her instincts had been correct. Harrison was a man in desperate need of love and she was the right woman for him. Only she could give it to him. Even if it couldn't be forever, he needed to feel, needed to know what it meant to understand love.

After leaving her mother's apartment, Lucia had thought of nothing else but freeing Harrison, of making him feel what she could give.

The need to love him had so consumed her that she'd created the heart earrings that had cried to be born from her artistic fingers. The tiny teardrop hearts graced her earlobes tonight.

As they moved toward the stage Lucia managed to catch Charles's gaze. He nodded, and Lucia created a spot for her and Harrison on the dance floor. His nod meant that the band would play a slow song before the end of the set, and Lucia couldn't wait. But for now, she'd settle for Harrison dancing with her even it was first to a faster number.

"Dance with me," she told him, and to his credit, Harrison managed to dance admirably well. He moved easily to the music, and Lucia laughed as he loosened up and let the rhythm flow through his body. With each beat of music he loosened and relaxed, undulating his body with the best dancers out on the floor.

"You're good," Lucia told him proudly. She'd known he would be, once he rediscovered in himself the potential that he'd locked away. She clapped her hands together as he executed a move that some young dancer next to him showed him how to do.

"I'll feel it in the morning," Harrison told her with a pleased laugh.

"You're feeling it now," Lucia told him, her delight in his companionship obvious. She put a hand on his chest and put one over her head. For a moment she danced as close as possible to him, and then she backed away.

Yes, she thought as she stared into his eyes, she wanted this man.

It wasn't supposed to happen this way, but wasn't that what always happened? People found each other when they weren't looking, and people didn't necessarily find what they thought they were looking for.

But when they found it, they knew it was perfect for them.

And that's what Harrison was. As Charles began the slower number, Lucia put both of her hands out to Harrison. Without words he drew her into his arms and close to his body.

Yes, she'd found a slice of heaven, Lucia thought as she rested her head upon his chest. His arms were strong, his chest steely and firm, and the fire that burned between them continued to flare hotter as they swayed together to the love song.

"You feel divine," she whispered, for she meant it. And, despite her ex-fiancé's claim that she was fast and loose, Lucia knew she wasn't. But she was a modern woman, and with Harrison, she knew she had to be forward. He wouldn't come to her; his sense of duty would forbid it.

Worse, if Easton found out, he would forbid it. Just as she'd told Hester, Lucia knew she needed to be careful. But the results would be so worth the risk.

"I think I need that water now," he told her when the song, and the set, had ended.

She smiled. "Certainly." Baby steps, but some kind of steps had to be made.

After they'd made a trip to the bar for glasses of

water, Lucia led Harrison over to where Charles and the band were resting.

"Hey, girlfriend," Charles greeted her.

"Charles," Lucia said. Placing her fingers lightly on Harrison's arm, she guided him forward. "Charles, this is Harrison."

"Great to meet you, man," Charles said. He took a long sip of water. "Whatcha think?"

"Very good," Harrison replied.

"I told you he'd like it." Lucia laughed. She playfully punched Charles's arm. "See."

"Ah, you're right once again. This is Lucky Lucia, did you know that? She predicted we'd be a smash when we just started out, and it's turning out that way."

"Their first single just hit number one on the Billboard chart," Lucia told Harrison proudly.

"Lucia's been there for us since the beginning," Charles said. "You're lucky, mate, if she chooses to latch on to you."

"Flatterer," Lucia said, giving Charles another playful punch. "Go get ready for your next set. I'll catch up with you later." She turned to Harrison.

"Is there a place we can talk?" he asked her.

She blinked. "It's quieter on the next level."

"Lead the way," Harrison said. He followed her easily, contemplating the disturbing thoughts running through his mind. The easy way Charles and Lucia had bantered made him experience a sharp, bitter pang, a feeling he hadn't really ever felt before. No, before Lucia he'd never truly experienced F. Scott Fitzgerald's green-eyed monster called jealousy.

But now he knew he'd fully experienced it, and Harrison knew the monster lived within him. He followed Lucia to a quiet table in a darker corner. He wanted answers.

"I've known Charles since he moved into my building two years ago," Lucia volunteered as they took their seats. "His fiancée is an old college buddy of mine."

"They live together?" Despite himself, relief filled him.

"Yes." Lucia nodded. "Of course, don't tell my mother that. She still thinks that Charles is after me or vice versa. That's why I brought him to the wedding."

"I thought he looked familiar."

"Exactly. I brought him because my mother usually disapproves of what she calls my 'inappropriate men.' I think I do it mainly to shock her."

"Your mother doesn't like your friends," Harrison stated. He found this concept intriguing. He'd never known Devon's friends well enough to know if he'd dislike them or not.

"My mother wants me to be in what a lot of my friends call 'upper-crust society.' I mean, I guess I am by virtue of my birth, but that doesn't mean that

I need to be a snob. I've been there done that with the debutante scene. I just prefer to hang out with what I see as real people, people to whom what a person looks like is not the deciding factor of whether they should be friends or not.''

"So you prefer being in the ordinary, everyday world of the common man."

"Absolutely." Lucia fingered her water glass. "I prefer the subway to taking a cab. I prefer the library to a bookstore. I like free concerts in Central Park better than going to balls. My mother thinks they must have dropped me on my head or something at the hospital."

Harrison looked mortified and Lucia laughed. "No, I'm teasing. I love my mother, and I know she loves me, but we've never been that close. She's into business and all the glam and glitter of wheeling and dealing. I just make jewelry."

"But you're famous for it."

"I just happen to be good. Being a Carradigne doesn't help in the artistic world. Sure, it might have opened a door or two and provided the initial loans for the purchase of raw materials, but either a person has talent or they don't. I'm a firm believer in that."

Harrison nodded. "I've seen men who come into the military who can't handle the regime, the pressure of being under someone else's orders."

"Exactly. See, you understand. It doesn't matter

who the person is, they either have the right stuff or they don't.''

"But you had to have some business sense," he said.

"Of course," she replied. "But that's secondary to my creative instinct. If I can't create, I have no business."

"So you like to move through the city with anonymity."

"Yes," she said. "I also refuse to be a celebrity just because of my lineage. Until Krissy's column, I could pretty much move about unrecognized. I'm still pretty safe, but with Grandfather in town it's getting a little more hairy."

Harrison instantly became protective. "You really should have personal security."

"I took a self-defense martial-arts class," she told him. "My mother insisted. I can take care of myself."

"I still don't like it," Harrison replied. He didn't either. There were factors at work that she didn't know about, or need to know about, until Easton determined it appropriate to tell her.

"Well, pretty soon I may have to give it up anyway," Lucia said, her expression turning wistful. "If I'm queen of Korosol I won't have a life of my own, will I?"

As Easton had told him, Harrison knew that in this situation only honesty would do. "No. Your first focus is on the country and the affairs of state. Your private life, and your personal life, is secondary. It's a sacrifice, but one that, if you are chosen, and if you are up to it, you will love."

"I don't know." With Harrison, Lucia suddenly felt comfortable expressing her doubts. "I know you've done it, but I've lived my life the way I've wanted to."

"Being a queen is being a total public figure," Harrison said. "But you have a great understanding of the common man. I can see that just from your relationships with people, and the ease with which you fit in here."

"I just don't know," she repeated.

Harrison felt compelled to put his hand over hers. Both comfort and strength could be found in his touch. "I think you would make a fantastic queen."

But at what cost? Lucia wondered. She kept that thought to herself. Now was not the time. "So tell me, Harrison, have you had regrets of your public service?"

Harrison thought for a moment. Mary was one, and so was Devon, but in the grand scheme of his life he had done so much more good. "No," he said. "I have no regrets."

Lucia looked as if she didn't quite believe his answer. "Not even in love?" Her voice was gentle as she placed her loose hand on top of the hand he'd captured hers with. "You can tell me."

"There was someone," he said finally.

"Your wife?"

"My wife," he replied.

"You loved her." It was a statement of fact.

"Actually," Harrison drew a long breath, "in retrospect I don't think I really did. Not with the passionate, I - can't - imagine - my - life - without - you, you're - my - other - half love. When Mary became pregnant she was seventeen."

"And you married her," Lucia said.

"Of course." Harrison nodded. "Korosol is much more conservative than America. I would never shirk my responsibilities."

"Of course you wouldn't," Lucia replied. She caressed the top of his hand lightly with her own. "That's one of the things that impresses me about you most. You have integrity. A lot of people my age or younger don't know what the word means."

"Thank you," Harrison replied. "But really, I don't deserve praise."

"You're modest as well." Lucia's tone showed her approval.

"No, I'm not." Harrison removed his hand. "While I may have learned not to regret what I've done, I'm not proud of it."

Lucia looked surprised. "I don't understand. Please explain. What did you do that was so horrible?"

"I'm a lousy father."

There—the words were out.

"That's impossible. Your son is such a credit to you, and he clearly adores you. I saw it for myself the other day when I was at the embassy."

"He was just being polite," Harrison said. "I think he always has blamed me for being gone so much. I often left him and his mother alone for weeks at a time. When Mary died I didn't know what to do with a son I'd hardly ever seen. We didn't speak much after he went to military school."

Lucia recaptured Harrison's hand. "Just remember, you have a future to rebuild your relationship."

Harrison looked into her eyes, seeing an intensity that hadn't been there before. He did have the future to rebuild his relationship with his son. Lucia's father had died when she was six. She'd never really had a chance to have a relationship with her own father.

The next music set began, and Harrison suddenly felt old. He could, after all, be Lucia's father. He didn't deserve her quiet strength, and worse, he couldn't let himself even desire her. But how he wanted to!

"Let's dance." At her words his head snapped up. Lucia was already on her feet, and her hands grasped his and pulled him to the dance floor.

"I really should be getting you home," he began, but Lucia's finger on his lips silenced him.

"Tonight, you live in my world," she told him. "Tonight, you are free."

Her tone was final, and so Harrison obeyed and let himself be free. For one night he danced, and best of all, he and Lucia spent hours talking in between band sets. The next time he looked at his watch it was 2:00 a.m.

Time had never gone so fast, or marked so pleasurable an evening. "I know, it's late," Lucia said with a slight apologetic smile.

"I have an early meeting at the embassy," Harrison said.

Lucia gave him a wry smile. "I'll dream of you while I'm sleeping in."

That image was almost too much to bear, and Harrison let out a little groan. Lucia laughed. "Come on, I know of a nice little all-night deli. Let's get a bite to eat. I'm starving."

Later, after splitting a delicious Reuben sandwich, complete with sauerkraut, Harrison finally hailed a cab to take them home.

At Lucia's building he stepped out and asked the driver to wait. He opened the door and assisted Lucia as she stepped onto the sidewalk. "So this is as wild as you get," he teased.

"This is it." Lucia's smile widened. "Would you like to come up and see my loft?"

Did he? Even though it was three-thirty in the morning, Harrison didn't want the evening to end.

Lucia's invitation told him that she didn't want it to end either.

He could read the longing in her face, see it in her body language and hear it in the tone of her voice. She wanted him, and so help him, he wanted her.

But he couldn't have her.

For even though Lucia claimed that for tonight he was free, he knew he wasn't. He was tied and bound, as always, to his duty to Korosol. And she was a princess, and nineteen years too young for him at that.

"Are you entering, Miss Carradigne?" the uniformed guard asked.

Lucia looked up at Harrison. *Am I?* she telepathically asked. "Are you going to see my loft?"

"Go on," Harrison told her softly. "I have an early meeting."

"I know that," Lucia said, playing off his refusal with infinite grace. "I meant later today. How about you come by at around five? You still need to see if I'm suitable."

She hid the date behind logic, and Harrison couldn't refuse, didn't want to refuse. The words slipped out, sealing his fate irrevocably. "I'll be here."

"Then it's not good-night or goodbye," Lucia said. "Just that I'll see you later." She reached forward and stroked his cheek again. Harrison closed his eyes, letting the beautiful feeling of her fingertips wash over him.

This much he could have. This much he could feel, could cherish, and he engraved it in his memory for later when the loneliness crept in.

Her hand lifted from his face and Harrison felt her step away before he opened his eyes. The uniformed guard opened the door, and with a small wave, Lucia stepped inside the building and soon disappeared from sight.

Harrison turned, entered the cab and endured the silent drive to the embassy as the magic ended.

Chapter Four

Lucia entered her loft, too keyed up and too on edge to simply go right to sleep. She'd been hit with a brainstorm in the elevator, and as always when work called her, she had to follow its inspiration.

As she crossed the large open room, she tossed her coat on the white leather sofa. Normally she would go straight to her workbench, pull out a fresh sheet of paper and start sketching. But not tonight.

Tonight she forced herself to get ready for bed before moving to her bookcases. She ran her fingers over her beloved volumes, searching for something specific, something she had filed away on a shelf long ago when she'd moved in. She'd been pulling the volume out a lot lately, especially when she made her sisters' wedding gifts.

There it was. *The History of Korosol.* Lucia pulled the oversize volume down and crossed the room. Within moments she'd made herself comfortable on her queen-size brass four-poster bed.

Despite her impatience to find what she was looking for, Lucia turned the pages slowly. As a girl she'd loved reading this book, and she'd memorized most of the historical stories.

If her mother had found it odd that Lucia was interested in the land of the Carradignes, Charlotte had never let on. But she hadn't let the girls ever visit Korosol after their father's death, and she hadn't needed much convincing to part with the book when Lucia had finally struck out on her own and found her own place to live.

Lucia paused at a black-and-white picture of her grandmother Cassandra. The image had been taken when Cassandra was twenty-two, and it was amazing how much Lucia's sister CeCe looked like her grandmother. For a moment Lucia wondered if her grandfather had seen the resemblance. Probably.

Finally Lucia found exactly what she was looking for. A smile crossed her face as she traced the emblem with her finger. Yes, she could craft this particular item easily. She closed her eyes and began to visualize, her fingers mentally working over the golden image. Within moments, she was fast asleep.

"LATE NIGHT?"

Harrison blinked and glanced toward the office doorway as Devon, looking more awake than his father felt, strolled in.

"Why do you say that?" Harrison avoided answering Devon's question by asking one of his own.

"Because it's 7:00 a.m. and you look tired," Devon said easily. "You never look tired." He sat down in a chair across from Harrison's desk and studied his father.

"You know King Easton is an early riser," Harrison replied with the skill of a practiced liar. He reached for the double espresso sitting in front of him and took a sip of the hot black liquid. He wasn't about to tell his son that yes, he'd only had about two hours of sleep. "I guess the stress of the king's mission to find an heir is starting to show on me."

"Speaking of that, how did the interview with Lucia go yesterday?"

Harrison masked his features. "Fine."

Devon arched an eyebrow at the abrupt answer. "Just fine?"

"I don't see Lucia Carradigne having skeletons in the closet like the other two sisters," Harrison replied easily. "She has some artsy-type friends who aren't the social norm, but that just indicates that she can move easily throughout the general population."

Devon nodded, buying Harrison's answer. "The king will be glad to hear that."

"I'm meeting with him for breakfast in a few minutes."

"Tell him I think I may have found Krissy's source, but I have no confirmation yet. Positive confirmation should be forthcoming."

"Good. The king wants this matter settled quickly."

"I think we all do," Devon said with a wry smile. "I'm ready to go home."

It was a rare admission, and Harrison stared at his son. They actually had something else in common, a longing for their mutual homeland. "I am ready, too," he said. "Although, I like New York. The people are resilient and strong, and this city teems with life and vigor."

"Still, New York doesn't hold a candle to Korosol," Devon said.

Harrison said nothing. It did hold a candle to Korosol. A large flame, actually. Lucia. He kept that thought to himself.

"I am starting to feel hemmed in," Devon admitted. "The sun never really reaches the sidewalks."

"I think Easton's ready to go home as well," Harrison said. "We've been here much longer than he ever anticipated when he planned this trip."

"Well, hopefully he will find Lucia suitable and we can all go home."

Harrison shifted in his chair. There was the paradox. As soon as Easton named Lucia his heir to the throne, Harrison could go home. But returning home to Korosol changed everything. It meant that he couldn't see Lucia anymore, except in an official capacity.

He frowned to himself. Where had that thought come from? He could only see Lucia now in an official capacity, right? Isn't that all the club last night was, his job? The job he loved?

Besides, didn't Easton want Lucia to fall in love with Devon? Shouldn't he be happy for his son?

Devon didn't seem to notice his father's sudden silence. "Just between us, when will he decide?"

"Who?" Harrison jolted from his thoughts. "Oh, Easton. I'm not sure when he'll decide or make the announcement. He hasn't yet privileged me with that information. When I do I'm sure that as captain of the Royal Guard you will be one of the first to know."

Devon stood. "Keep me informed."

"I'll do that, and I'll give Easton your update about Krissy Katwell."

"Thank you." With that, Devon was gone.

Harrison glanced at his Rolex. He still had a minute before he needed to leave for Easton's office.

Exactly what would he tell the king?

ONE HOUR LATER the answer was set in stone.

He'd told Easton he'd need more time.

As Harrison stepped into the elevator, he contemplated the conversation. He mulled over what he'd done. The lie had slipped out, and Harrison himself couldn't really believe it. Never before had he lied this outright, or this much, to his king.

But Easton had been so ready to name Lucia the successor, so excited at the prospect, that Harrison had found himself in a rare state of panic mixed with the desire to protect.

King Easton had wanted to make the announcement today. He'd wanted a press conference set for two that afternoon.

Harrison understood the king's reasoning. With all the press leaks, Easton didn't want his subjects to learn about their new queen from a tabloid gossip column. While Easton preferred to make the announcement in Korosol, the leaks made that impossible. Time was of the essence.

So Harrison had lied—something he'd been doing a lot lately since meeting Lucia.

But deep down, Harrison knew that Lucia wasn't ready for King Easton's announcement. At least not yet. Last night during one of their many conversations she'd told Harrison about certain things she wanted to do in the next few weeks. For Lucia, being named queen would make doing these things impossible.

So, when Easton had asked Harrison what the results of the investigation were, Harrison had told

Easton that he'd have the full report one week from Sunday at the latest. That would give Lucia time to prepare, to wrap up any loose ends.

And it would give him a week.

A week for what he wasn't sure, but for the first time in his life, Harrison knew he had to give himself time to find out.

"If it isn't the great Sir Montcalm, hero to the realm."

Harrison turned, concentration broken. He stiffened upon seeing the owner of the annoying voice. This was one man he broke protocol for by refusing to bow or use his title. "Markus," Harrison said coldly.

"Has the king finally made up his mind?" This question came from Winston, Markus's ever-present shadow who currently lurked to Markus's right.

"The king often makes up his mind," Harrison said with the evasiveness of a skilled tactician. "Is there a specific matter you are referring to?"

Markus gave a short laugh. "Come, Winston. We shouldn't waste our time. You know Sir Montcalm is no more than the king's puppet on a golden string, incapable of thinking for himself."

"Yes, he's lucky you aren't king. He'd be out of a job. You prefer people with brains."

Then what's he doing with you? Harrison wanted

to shoot back. He bit his tongue to keep that reply from slipping out. He would not let his control slip.

Harrison exhaled the breath he'd been holding as he watched them walk away. The more he saw Markus, the more he was certain of it. The man was a wolf in sheep's clothing.

In fact, Harrison knew that Markus was pure evil.

He just wished that he had proof, something besides his gut instinct to go on.

"MISS CARRADIGNE IS expecting you," the doorman said as Harrison gave his name to the uniformed gentleman standing outside the entrance to Lucia's loft. "Take the freight elevator to the top floor. You'll need to buzz the apartment to get the elevator to go up."

"Thank you," Harrison said. He followed the point of the man's white-gloved finger and bypassed the lobby elevators. He turned down a small hall, and soon was in a private, express freight elevator.

He pushed the button by the intercom, but instead of a human voice answering, another buzz sounded and the elevator doors simply slid open. Harrison stepped inside. The elevator was plain, nothing like the posh ones at the embassy or Charlotte's apartment. Within moments, he found himself whisked up the express elevator that only stopped on Lucia's floor.

When the elevator door opened, he was standing directly in Lucia's loft.

Immediately he could see that it was, well, for lack of a better word, her.

The loft was synonymous with Lucia. Tall columns divided living spaces and held up twenty-four-foot-high ceilings. Floor-to-ceiling windows allowed light to pour in from every angle. From her vantage point, from the top floor of the apartment building the city didn't seem so dark. In fact, Lucia had a panoramic view that included the Hudson River off in the distance.

Speaking of Lucia, Harrison's gaze searched the open spaces for her. She hadn't come to greet the elevator, but he knew she was home. Classical music filtered through the hidden stereo speakers, and Harrison paused for a moment.

He recognized the artist, Vladimir Horowitz playing a Mozart piano concerto. A smile crept across his face.

His Lucia was full of surprises.

He turned slightly, and this time found himself facing her bedroom, or at least the area that held her bed. She didn't really have a bedroom. Instead, she had an area with a large four-poster bed that was separated from the main living space by a series of smaller architectural columns.

She had topped her brass bed with a spread of white lace, a contrast to the more modern feel of the rest of the loft. Her bed looked soft, romantic, inviting.

Harrison pivoted. He didn't need to think about that. He shifted his gaze, bypassing Lucia's couches. The kitchen area that jutted into the room was a stainless-steel workplace that would be any chef's culinary delight. He searched on, hoping to find her in another area of the loft.

Ah, there she was.

He frowned slightly. She had her back to him. Odd. Lucia was not the type to ignore someone. She had buzzed him up, hadn't she?

Disconcerted, Harrison strode forward, his footsteps quiet, yet still audible so as not to scare her. As he approached he noticed that her head was bent over as if she was concentrating on something. Her shoulders moved as if she was working on something with her hands. Her blond hair hid her face from his view.

Sudden insight hit him, and Harrison slowed his approach. She was at her workbench, deep in concentration from working on something. As her fingers put it down, he took a good look at the golden object. While he didn't know what piece of jewelry she was creating, he knew what it represented. It was the Korosolan symbol for honor.

"Hey," Lucia said. She stretched her arms forward and turned her head from side to side as if to stretch out her neck. "I lost track of time."

"No problem," Harrison said, realizing he meant the words. Normally people who were late drove him crazy. "I enjoyed watching you create. What type of piece are you working on?"

"A tie tack," Lucia said. She picked up the pin and turned it over in her fingers before handing the piece to him. "Here, you can see it."

As she passed him the pin, their fingertips connected and Harrison felt a frisson of electricity pass through him. Lucia Carradigne was magical, of that he was certain. She'd lost track of time to create something so unique, so special.

What made it even better was that Harrison could see how meticulous and focused she had been on her work. He admired commitment and work ethic. Once again, he'd discovered that there were many sides to the multifaceted young woman.

He was discovering he liked her more and more each and every time he saw her.

He held the pin, sensing the warmth coming from the metal.

"Wonderful work," he told her.

Her cheeks flushed a little, as if his comment was somehow extra special. "Thank you," Lucia said. She pushed a blond hair out of her face. "I'm not quite finished yet, but I was hit with inspiration last night and I had to start on the piece immediately."

He found that concept interesting, considering

she hadn't gotten home until the wee hours of the morning. "Do you often work from inspiration?"

"All the time," she replied. "I find my inspiration everywhere, and last night I couldn't get right to sleep until I began researching this project."

Harrison was further impressed. Judging from the creations on her workbench, she had many pieces in process. "So I assume that you work on multiple projects at one time."

"Always. Somehow I even manage to get them all done on time, which still amazes me. Somehow I always finish whatever I start."

"Amazing," Harrison said, for to him it was. "I have to do one task at a time, or make lots of to-do lists."

"I hate to-do lists," Lucia replied with a shudder. "While I admire those who can use them, I find myself getting frustrated by them. I think that they limit me." She laughed suddenly, her voice sounding like tinkling bells to Harrison's ears. "But then, I'm not the world's most organized person."

Harrison's lips arched up into a small, wry smile. "I think I'm overorganized. It's almost a flaw," Harrison said.

"Oh, I doubt that," Lucia reassured. "Organization and getting things done are two of your strengths, and really something that I admire about you."

He shot her a quizzical look, encouraging her to

continue. He'd never heard himself described quite in this manner before.

"Seriously." She nodded. "How else would you handle the demands of a king and a kingdom? You've found what works for you and I admire that. I respect a person who finds what works for them and sticks with it."

Taken off guard by her praise, Harrison didn't know what to say, so he simply said, "Thank you."

"You're welcome," Lucia said with a wide smile that made the corner of her eyes crinkle delightfully. "Isn't it interesting how people can be so unique and different yet still so the same? Opposites can attract, and even better, get along because we build on each other's strengths. Just think of the combination we'd make."

Her words, delivered so innocently, hit him like a lightning bolt. Here was a woman who barely knew him, yet she intuitively understood him.

He studied her, seeing again the inner beauty that made the surface beauty of Lucia shine even more. Lucia radiated an inner serenity that somehow made Harrison feel more at home than he had been in his marriage, or even at the Korosolan palace.

While he and Easton were friends, Harrison wasn't royalty, and that invisible line dividing them was always present.

And the difference between Lucia and Mary

couldn't have been clearer. Take the to-do lists, for example.

Mary had found his to-do lists annoying, and her derision for Harrison's orderly life had her often sneering at his use of them. She'd even gone so far as to claim that anyone who couldn't function without a list ought to have his or her head examined.

Lucia, while admitting she found to-do lists limiting, had with just a few words from her perfect lips reaffirmed her belief in the lists' validity. In essence, she'd told Harrison she found it not a weakness, but one of his strengths, one that complemented her inability to use them.

"So how did your meeting go with Easton?" she asked. She reached her hand forward and Harrison placed the pin back in her palm. He assumed she was making the tie tack for her grandfather. He knew Easton would be pleased. Honor was important to him. He'd often declared it a man's greatest strength.

"My meeting went well," Harrison said.

"Did he want to know when he could make an announcement?" The quiver in Lucia's voice was almost imperceptible, but Harrison heard it. Immediately Harrison knew he'd made the right decision in what he'd told Easton.

"He did," Harrison told her. As he watched, her lips parted and she tucked the bottom one under two of her top teeth. Yes, he'd made the correct choice, even if it had involved stretching the truth. "I told him I needed another week."

Lucia's delight was almost that of an exuberant child. Her face broke into a wide smile and she moved forward. She tossed her arms around Harrison and gave him a big hug. "Thank you."

Despite himself and the fact that he knew he should extract himself from her warm grip, Harrison instead drew her further into his arms.

She felt perfect, as if she'd been made to fit next to him. He'd noticed that detail during the short dance they'd shared at CeCe's reception. He'd noticed it last night. Now, like those nights, her cheek pressed against his chest, and they stood there in silence for a moment.

Heaven couldn't have been any sweeter.

A timer's buzzing interrupted the magical moment, and Lucia pulled back. She smiled wistfully. "Dinner's ready," she said.

"I am hungry," he replied, a bit relieved. The extent of his need and craving for her overwhelmed him. All that desire from just a hug. He'd do well to stay farther away and avoid touching her.

"I'm glad you're hungry, because I actually cooked dinner instead of cheating and just warming up carryout," Lucia told him.

"You cooked for me?" Harrison couldn't remember when someone besides the palace chef had actually made him a special meal, which usually entailed just heating up leftovers from a banquet.

"I like cooking," Lucia said. "I just never have anyone to cook for unless I host small dinner parties for my friends. Unfortunately they're usually too busy to do anything but eat and run. I know you probably think that at my age I'm this flirty young socialite always out partying, but in reality I'm not out that much. I'd opt to have a quiet evening at home anytime."

"I never thought you were a flirty socialite," Harrison protested as he followed her to the kitchen area.

"Sure you did," Lucia said. Pressing a button, she turned the timer off. "That first time we met. I could see it in your eyes."

"Well, maybe a little," Harrison admitted. "But in reality I wondered why a beautiful woman such as yourself was asking an old man like me to dance."

"Because in my eyes you weren't an old man, but a very attractive man that I was dying to meet." Lucia's green eyes reflected her frankness. She put a pair of pot holders on her hands.

"To be honest, Harrison, in general I'm pretty distrustful of men, especially after that gold-digger fiancé I had the misfortune of having. But something about you draws me to you, despite the risk."

"Risk?"

"You could be the type I could fall very hard for." And with those words, Lucia turned her back to him and reached inside the oven.

Her words resonating in his ears, Harrison sat down on the black leather-topped stainless-steel bar stool. Warmth spread through his veins.

He could be the type she could fall very hard for. Then, as if a bucket of cold water had doused him, a chill iced over every pore of his skin.

She could fall for him. She was a princess, soon to be heir to the Korosolan throne.

As much as it was heaven to hear her words, and heaven to simply hold her, God forbid his desire. He did desire her, fiercely. He wanted nothing more than to take her into his arms and kiss her. But he couldn't. Lucia Carradigne was forbidden.

Off-limits. Taboo.

She was not his to have.

Easton had made it perfectly clear to everyone that he'd marked her for Devon. And to defy his king... It was bad enough he'd lied. He already compromised so much.

She stood up, a stoneware pan of steaming lasagna in her hands. The smell wafting to his nostrils was nothing short of wonderful.

"If you'd follow me, dinner is served," Lucia said.

And with that, Harrison followed her to a small table for two. From their vantage point next to the windows, they could see the last slivers of sunlight vanish from the April sky.

"This is excellent," Harrison told her after his first bite of the delicious pasta.

"Mama Rosina's secret recipe," she said. "Authentic from Little Italy. She cleans my loft and I traded the recipe for some earrings she saw on my workbench."

"I think you were the winner in that trade," Harrison said as he sipped his glass of Merlot. He'd refused at first, saying he was on duty. But Lucia had insisted he at least have one glass, if only to complement the flavor of the food. He was having difficulty refusing her anything, and this was so minor. Besides, after following a bite of lasagna with the wine, Harrison agreed. She'd been right on the wine, and with the meal.

She'd created a dinner that was a culinary delight to his palate.

"I think I made a pretty good deal, too," Lucia replied. With a twist of her wrist she forked some spinach salad greens into her mouth. "I'm usually pretty lucky in bartering for things. It's an old art, but in this part of town, definitely not dead."

"I don't think I've ever bartered for goods," Harrison said. He tried to think back and remember if there had actually been a time.

"You're a negotiator and you've never bartered?" She shook her head in disbelief.

"Well, sure. Bartering is common for political alliances and financial matters perhaps, but for a recipe, no. I think I'd just buy the cookbook and make do."

"Or you'd just order carryout."

"That, too," Harrison agreed with a laugh, ignoring the fact that as the king's adviser he more often than not had meals at the palace. "And I know I simply just go to the store and buy things. Maybe I negotiate so much that I want my shopping straightforward."

"Haggling is part of the fun," Lucia said. "It's almost a hobby of mine. So do you have any?" Seeing his expression, she waved a fork at him. "Hobbies, I mean. Surely you must have some."

Did he? Harrison thought for a moment. When was the last time he'd even had an actual vacation? He couldn't remember. "I like to fish," he said finally. "But I don't often get away much to do it. And I read. I get a lot of time to do that, especially when I'm in an airplane or waiting for King Easton."

Lucia nodded, her understanding evident. "Your job consumes you."

"It does," he agreed with a slight incline of his head. "Many have told me that it's my curse." Including Mary. She'd hated his job and eventually would have divorced him if she hadn't died suddenly.

"Work can be a curse only if you let it become one," Lucia replied easily. She set her fork down, her salad finished. "I think having a job you love is actually more of a blessing. My job is my hobby, and my hobby is my job. I couldn't imagine doing anything else, and so what if it consumes me? It makes me happy."

Again the contrast between Mary and Lucia was staggering and he took a minute to study Lucia. While he'd known she was a unique woman, now he was even more certain of that fact.

"I thought I was the only one who felt that way," Harrison said.

"You're not," Lucia said with a vigorous shake of her head that sent her blond hair into her face. She pushed it back. "Believe me, I understand. However, I wish my mother did. There's no way she'll ever understand why I've turned down society balls just to work on what she calls my 'trivial' jewelry."

"Your jewelry isn't trivial." It shocked Harrison to think that Charlotte would have said that.

"No, not to me. However, my mother isn't pleased with my choice of career. It isn't like I make enough of a fortune to please her. Hence, she just wants me married to a man she deems appropriate," Lucia said. "What I happen to want is irrelevant, especially since I'm not involved in the family firm."

"That's archaic," Harrison said. Then he sobered. "Although, who am I to pass judgment? I married Mary because it was the right thing to do."

Lucia leaned forward a little, her face intense. "No one can ever think less of you for that. You did what you felt was right, and few people have that quality or that commitment to their code of honor. As for love, you just haven't found your soul mate yet, that's all. I'm sure you will."

Harrison's lips twisted in a wry smile. "I'm a little too old to believe in finding a soul mate."

"Please." Lucia put up a hand as if to halt his negative thoughts. "Enough with calling yourself old. I don't want to hear it in my presence again." She straightened up and looked him directly in the eye. "Got it?"

"Is that a royal command?" Seeing how serious her expression was, Harrison couldn't resist teasing her to lighten the mood.

She relaxed with another wide smile. "Yes, as a matter of fact, it is. That's right, I do have the authority to give you orders, don't I?"

"That you do," Harrison said, knowing that while the word riddles they spoke were true, their intent in using them was not serious.

"Excellent." Lucia drew her chin up in mock stubbornness. "Then I hereby order you to start thinking of yourself as younger, especially when

you're around me. Because that's how I see you."
Her green eyes twinkled.

"Any other orders?"

"Oh, yes," Lucia said, warming to her topic. Her
eyelids lowered seductively. "I have plenty of other
orders I'm planning on giving you. But, you'll have
to wait to find out what they are."

His eyebrows arched. So this was how she
wanted to play it. He didn't mind. For once he actually wanted to play along. Lucia was fun, invigorating, and for the first time in years he felt truly
alive. Deliberately he let his own words hang out
there. "So I'll have to wait?"

"At least until after dessert," Lucia teased. She
stood and crossed the room. Opening the stainless-
steel refrigerator, she removed some tall glasses
filled with a dark brown froth. "I hope you like it.
I made chocolate mousse."

"From Mama Rosina's recipe?" he asked as she
came back to the table.

"No, from Hester's." As she placed the dessert
in front of Harrison, Lucia mentioned her mother's
housekeeper. "This was my favorite recipe as a
child, and I was always begging her to make it. I
think she got tired of my requests, because she
taught me how to make the dessert when I was
nine."

"Did she also teach you how to cook?"

"I'm pretty much the only one she let into the

kitchen,'' Lucia confirmed as she sat back down. "CeCe and Amelia made too much of a mess.''

"Somehow I can't see that,'' Harrison said. "Your sisters don't strike me as menaces to a kitchen.''

"Believe me, they are. Or at least they were, growing up. CeCe was always in the kitchen pretending to run the world and Amelia was always trying to save it from her. I just wanted to cook.''

"That could have driven anyone crazy,'' Harrison agreed. He liked the image of the young Carradigne girls playing in the kitchen.

"Anyway, Hester is close to all of us, but she really babied me because I was the youngest. I think it's also because I was six when my mother took over running the company right after my father died. CeCe and Amelia, at age nine and seven, weren't much older.''

"What does Hester think of your jewelry?''

"She was there at my grand opening.''

Lucia's green eyes twinkled as she remembered the event. "My mother didn't really give much support to what she saw as just a hobby she hoped I'd grow out of. Anyhow, I arranged my own big launch at this obscure art gallery just around the corner from here.''

"So did your mother attend?''

"Oh, she did.'' Lucia laughed slightly. "But what impressed me most was that Hester put on her finest and showed up. Hester tries to avoid stuff like that. She'll tell you she only puts on her best for weddings and funerals.''

''So your mother and Hester both were there.''

''Yes, and if my mother seemed a bit put out that her housekeeper was in attendance at something other than a wedding or a funeral, she didn't let on. I think my mother was too mortified with all my artsy friends who showed up in black leather and chains.''

Harrison smiled. ''I could see that about Charlotte.''

''I think she was sure that someone was going to rob her or something,'' Lucia said. ''Of course, none of that happened, but I know she was thinking it. She left pretty quickly after what she'd deemed was an appropriate appearance time.''

''So do you still do a lot of shows?''

''Much to my mother's relief, I'm now only in what she terms 'finer' art galleries,'' Lucia said. ''I think that first show mortified her so much that afterward she called a few friends of hers. But while she may have paved the way a little bit, my work did have to stand on its own merit. New York's art community is tough.''

''Of course your work stood on its own,'' Harrison stated. ''Just because you're a Carradigne doesn't mean people will simply humor you.''

''Especially since I'm not in the family firm.''

She twirled her spoon in the mousse and then put it in her mouth. To Harrison, her simple innocent movement bordered on erotic. "It's strange. Most of my work now is done through private referrals, but occasionally I still do a show. In fact, I have one this upcoming Thursday in Aspen, Colorado. I wasn't sure whether to cancel or not because of King Easton, but I decided to go ahead. The celebrity set is there for some late snow skiing and a gallery owner called me. She's an old friend who has believed in me since I started designing, so I agreed to do the show as a favor for her."

"I didn't know you were leaving town." Harrison spooned a bite of mousse into his mouth. The decadent chocolate flavor melted upon impact with his tongue, and for a brief moment he felt the stirrings of sensual ecstasy. He pushed the thoughts aside. He didn't need to think about eating Lucia's mousse that way.

"So when do you leave?" he asked.

"You mean when do *we* leave?" Lucia replied with a wicked smile.

Chapter Five

Harrison's head shot up and his gaze connected with hers. She spooned another bite into her mouth as if she knew the movement bothered him. "What are you talking about?" he asked.

"You are coming with me to Aspen." Her face showed how serious, and how obviously pleased with the idea, she was. "Seriously. I want you to come as part of your investigation into whether I'm suitable or not. It's the perfect opportunity for you to see me in action outside of New York. Besides, you are the one who says I need to step up the security surrounding me. While precautions have been taken, I will be surrounded by lots of valuable jewelry."

Her logic made sense, but deep down he sensed the real reason. And deep down he wanted to be with her as she seemed to want him. He opened his mouth in an attempt to buy time. "I'll—"

Lucia interrupted him. "No, don't even say

you'll think about it. Don't even say it's Devon's job. Just say you'll go. Be impulsive for once. Besides, Aspen had late snow, so we can ski. You do ski, don't you?''

"Yes," Harrison said. He'd often skied in the Larella Mountains of Korosol. Was that a hobby? Maybe he did have a few more than he'd originally thought.

"Great. We'll ski. I'm sure you'll need to make sure I can do that, especially so I don't embarrass myself in front of the press. I mean, if the press follows Prince Charles and his sons when they ski, they'll probably start following me all over Europe once my grandfather names me his heir, right?"

With that argument delivered, Lucia stood and began to clear the dishes off the table. She carried the dirty plates into the kitchen. As she placed the dishes in the sink, she smiled to herself. He'd say yes, she knew it.

Her female intuition told her that Harrison, despite his attempts to the contrary, wanted her.

And she wanted him. A great deal.

How and when she'd fallen for him didn't matter. She wanted this man, and for the little amount of time left before her life became a public spectacle, she wanted to spend it with him.

It was just convincing Harrison that he wanted the same that would be the challenge.

Lucia finished loading the dishes into the dishwasher and poured herself another glass of wine. If Hester was right, that the way to a man's heart was his stomach, then Lucia should be well on her way to Harrison's by now. She certainly hoped so.

From across the expanse of the loft, from behind the safety of her kitchen sink, she studied him. Didn't he know how attractive he was?

The military cut of his dark brown hair framed his classic face perfectly. From what she could tell from the moments in his arms, he was incredibly fit. Plus, those hazel eyes of his always seemed to be able to see into her soul.

Couldn't the man see what a knockout to women he was? Why did he doubt himself?

She frowned slightly as she pondered those questions. Pushing a strand of her dark blond hair out of her face, she decided that maybe he really didn't know. He'd been seventeen when he'd married his wife because of duty. He probably never would have married her if he hadn't gotten her pregnant.

Lucia straightened and took another sip of wine. Yes, his marriage hadn't been one of love, but of duty. A sudden insight hit her. He'd never really loved anyone then, and perhaps he didn't know how to let himself.

She hadn't really loved anyone either, but she knew what it wasn't. And since what she had with Harrison was nothing like what it wasn't, Lucia's artistic logic told her that what they could have, even briefly, could be the real kind of love that the lucky few found.

She smiled to herself as her emotional side mulled over that thought. Whatever this feeling was that she was having for Harrison, it wasn't like the sisterly feelings she had for his son, Devon.

Lucia's smile vanished and she sighed. Sir Devon Montcalm had been on her mind lately, and it hadn't been because she found him sexy or attractive. He was both of those, but she just wasn't interested, and deep down, she didn't think he was interested in her, either.

She'd have to ask Harrison how best to handle that annoying situation. She didn't want to offend her grandfather, but she did wish he'd stop throwing Devon at her at every opportunity. Her grandfather's matchmaking was about as subtle as her mother's, and had become equally unwelcome.

Why couldn't they leave her alone? She'd found someone suitable, someone much better for her. Now all she had to do was convince Harrison himself.

As she stole another glance at him, something told her that convincing him would be an uphill battle.

For while she suspected that Harrison felt the same way about her, he would never act on it. He'd be afraid of defying the king's wishes. After all, Easton's matchmaking was almost a royal edict.

Yes, she would have to make the first move, even if it meant looking like the fast-and-loose woman Gregory Barrett had accused her of being.

But she'd have to risk it. She didn't have time to take it nice and slow, although with Harrison she wanted to. But like Audrey Hepburn's character of the princess in the movie *Roman Holiday,* Lucia knew that time wasn't on her side. She'd soon be in the public eye, and Harrison would simply fade away, out of her life.

She only had now.

Now was all she had to create memories of a true love that would need to sustain her the rest of her life.

"Would you like another glass of wine?" she called.

"Water, please," Harrison said. Lucia smiled as she poured him a glass. The man was a model of restraint, and she'd predicted his answer.

Oh yes, Harrison, she thought. I know you, and you know me. Let's now take this to the next level. Time to loosen you up.

She brought her wineglass and his water goblet over to the sofa where he was now sitting thumbing through an issue of *National Geographic Traveler.* Lucia loved travel magazines, for through them she'd vicariously seen the world.

Other than that, she hadn't traveled much. Her mother hadn't really had the time for long family vacations, and once Lucia started out on her own, she hadn't the time either.

"By the way," she called, "thanks for being understanding and letting me finish the dishes. If I don't do them right away they'll sit for weeks."

Deliberately she touched her fingertips to his as she handed him his glass of water.

His eyes darkened from the sensation, and Lucia's stomach fluttered as if a garden of butterflies had opened their wings to the rising sun. He wanted her.

Let me be the one to love you, she told him mentally as he sipped his water and moved slightly out of her proximity.

"So, have you cleared this trip to Aspen with Easton?" he asked suddenly.

"You think I need to?" Lucia had never needed to clear a trip with anyone before. While waiting for Harrison's answer, she deliberately moved back into his proximity by pulling her legs up onto the sofa.

Her feet were bare, her toes painted with a muted red polish. Unless he moved to the other end of the couch, Harrison couldn't shift any farther away.

"Probably," he said, his tension at her nearness obvious.

"True." She cocked her head and looked at him while she contemplated that thought. "I guess you couldn't just disappear for a few days, could you?"

"No." Harrison shook his head, and winced slightly. "I think I slept wrong last night."

Fate delivered the opportunity Lucia had been waiting for. She now had her opening.

"Here. Lean forward." She slid behind him, placing her body behind his. Within moments she slid her fingers over the back of his neck.

Oh God. Lucia almost said the words aloud now that she had her fingers finally touching him. Under her fingers his skin felt so good, and desire rippled through her. *Feel it too,* she telepathically told him as she rubbed out the coiled tension evident in his neck muscles.

Verbally though, the loft was in silence as she kneaded gently, pressing lightly, then firmer as Harrison's head slid forward to allow her better access to his neck and shoulders.

She slid her hands into his hair, running them through the short strands of the military cut. She moved her fingers forward, sliding the tips over his temples. She leaned forward, pressing her body into his back as she massaged his forehead.

She felt him shudder slightly as she ran her fingers across his eyebrows. Her fingers traced the soft arching hairs in reverse. Slowly she touched, going in toward the bridge of his nose from the edge of his eyes. Then her fingers slid down his nose, and finally she butterflied her touch out over his lips.

His mouth parted under her ministrations, and

Lucia simply touched his lips, and felt them quiver, before she continued her hands' journey down his chin. His skin lacked telltale stubble, indicating he'd shaved before coming over for dinner. Lucia liked that. A lot. Harrison was so considerate.

Slowly she stroked the front of his neck before sliding her fingers back around to begin the process over again.

Love me, she told him mentally.

DANGER SIGNALS resounded loudly in Harrison's head, but for the first time in his life he refused to heed their warning.

Whatever magic flowed from Lucia Carradigne's fingertips had overridden any logical part of his brain. His cerebrum had simply shut down all thinking processes. The only work Harrison's brain could do right now was to let his body feel.

And what he felt was pure heaven, pure bliss, pure joy.

The wonder drug that was named Lucia had invaded his veins and lifted him to some other place, some other world where just the now existed, where their desire for each other could run free.

As if sensing his capitulation to his needs, to his desire, Lucia shifted. Never breaking contact with his body, she moved around and soon straddled his lap.

Facing him she eased down slowly, as if afraid

she'd hurt him when their bodies connected. Then her hands found the side of his face.

Harrison's gaze connected with hers and he drowned in her smoky green pools.

She was a mythical sorceress, the stuff of many Korosolan legends, and she'd come for him.

Even if it meant certain death, he couldn't resist her. No, he couldn't resist or deny the overpowering feelings he had just for her.

And so he waited. The seconds of time seemed like aeons of eternity as her lips, like the softest of petals falling from a rose, descended to meet his.

At the first touch of her flesh, he tasted the honey of her silken lips, and he shuddered with the awe-inspiring power of it. She pressed her lips gently to his, teasing, gently lifting away before fluttering back down to kiss him again.

His eyes closed and he let the blackness of not seeing her image intensify the feelings she was creating, feelings so overpowering and immense that he knew he'd never felt their like before.

Following her lead, he parted his lips and let her inside to create whatever further magic she would.

Whatever she wanted, whatever she needed, at this moment it was hers. His veins turned molten.

He'd give her anything, everything in his power, and even the things that weren't. He'd find a way.

Such was the magic, such was the desire, and

such was the ecstasy and sensation in something so simple as just her kiss.

And then, as she kissed him, his male body remembered its own role in the relationship between the sexes. Of their own volition, for his brain certainly wasn't thinking about what it was doing, his fingers slid into her hair.

Silk and satin strands touched his skin, and he arched his neck to give her access as her kisses moved across his chin and then over to his left ear. The light breath she blew into it caused a lower part of him to strain in a way it had never before.

"I want you," she whispered, and at her vocalization of her needs, he shattered.

Restraint gone, he pulled her back to his lips and crushed hers to his. "Yes," somehow he heard her say as his mouth took charge of the seduction and drank hers again with renewed thirst.

She tasted of wine, of chocolate mousse, and of all those things female that blended together to form nirvana. His tongue traced her teeth, traced the roof of her mouth, and mated with her as if he'd never touched, tasted or teased any other woman before.

They shifted, and holding his weight off of her, Harrison laid her back onto the white leather sofa. No words were needed as he planted kisses over her face.

He traced her eyebrows, the soft golden lashes

framing her green eyes, and kissed his way down her perfect nose. He flicked his tongue lightly and delicately over her jawline before sliding his lips' kisses farther down her smooth neck.

She emitted a little kittenish cry and arched to turn her neck, thus sending his kisses over and down the opposite side.

"You wore this to tempt me," he said, his breath ragged as he slid the strap of the sleeveless top aside.

"I always work in comfortable clothes," she said, her hands in his hair and on his neck as he planted kisses at the hollow of her throat.

"I'm a doomed man then," he said, moving his kisses to underneath where the strap had lain.

"I want you to be," she said, arching her back and sending his lips lower.

A shrill bell of warning went off in Harrison's brain as his lips lowered to the valley between her breasts and reached closer to their intended target.

"Damn," the unladylike curse word flew from Lucia's mouth and Harrison realized the annoying sound, which had ceased, had been the ringing of the phone.

"Lucia? Are you home?" On the answering machine, Harrison heard Easton's all-too-familiar, and right now very unwelcome, voice.

The thought registered again. Easton's voice. Lucia was his granddaughter. Harrison had been kissing Easton's granddaughter, a woman young enough to be his own daughter, if Devon's age was anything to go by.

"You need to get the phone." His tone was brusque, signaling the end of the magical moment. This was reality. Whatever place they'd slipped away to, for even that short wondrous time, wasn't reality.

It was an aberration, never able to happen again.

Lucia shifted, her displeasure at the telephone's interruption and Harrison's withdrawal from her obvious. She picked up the receiver, cutting off the machine. "Hello?"

"Lucia!" Her grandfather's voice boomed through the line so loudly that Harrison could hear it from where he sat composing himself on the other end of the sofa.

"Hello, Grandfather," Lucia said. She ran her fingers through her hair. "How are you?"

She paused, as if listening. "Uh-huh. I'm fine," she replied.

Harrison watched Lucia for a moment. She made the required noises at what Easton was saying, but Harrison could tell Lucia wasn't truly into the conversation.

Already he'd divided her from her grandfather, a grandfather she barely knew. Guilt crept through him. Easton was his friend, and if Easton knew what had been occurring right before his phone call...

Friendship or no, if Easton found out, Harrison would find himself out of a job and tossed out of his beloved Korosol faster than flies swarmed a picnic. Easton wanted to have Devon with Lucia, thus having a young royal couple to take Korosol into the future.

He never should have let the situation get this out of control. So help him, he was a grown man of forty-five, not a randy young teenager.

Being a randy teenager had gotten Mary pregnant.

He rose to his feet.

Seeing Harrison stand, Lucia's gaze suddenly pleaded with him. The message she sent was clear; she wanted him to stay. Harrison turned a blind eye to it. He shouldn't be here any longer. He shouldn't have been here in the first place.

"Thanks for dinner," he began to mouth, trying to be polite.

"Could you hold on for a moment?" Lucia asked her grandfather.

Harrison took a step toward the door, and Lucia, holding the phone to her ear, stood. Seeing her stricken face, he panicked.

For the first time in his life, Harrison Montcalm became a coward.

There was no way he could resist Lucia Carradigne. So, when faced with a battle he couldn't win, Harrison reverted to his training as a general in the Korosolan Army.

He could not surrender. Thus, he made a hasty retreat, and fled.

Chapter Six

He'd left. As Lucia watched the elevator doors close, she couldn't believe it. Then again, yes she could. Her grandfather's timing with his phone call left quite a lot to be desired.

What had Easton been saying anyhow? She tried to focus, the subject of her thoughts—Harrison—already at the ground floor, according to the numbers above the elevator.

"Lucia, I need an answer. Did you hear me?" Easton asked.

"Huh?" Lucia said. "I'm sorry. Could you repeat that?"

She heard her grandfather sigh and knew she had disappointed him with her lack of attention.

"Yes," he said. "Charlotte and I are hosting a dinner party tomorrow night for family and my close staff. We both thought it would be a good opportunity for you and Devon to become closer."

No wonder she hadn't wanted to listen. Her

grandfather's words were just wonderful. *Not.* Once again he and her mother had put together another matchmaking attempt. Just what Lucia didn't need right at this time in her life. Not when she had her relationship, if she could even call it that, with Harrison to worry about.

"I'm very busy right now, Grandfather," Lucia said. "I have a jewelry show in Aspen and I need to finish a few pieces."

Easton wasn't pleased. "What do you mean a jewelry show?"

"I have a showing at an art gallery in Aspen, Colorado, Thursday. I need to finish up a few special pieces that the owner requested I bring." She hoped her grandfather would take the hint.

He didn't. "Can't someone else finish them for you? I'd like you to be here."

Lucia checked her impatience. She had to remember that her grandfather, surrounded by a personal staff, didn't know how she worked. Unlike other designers, she didn't employ a staff. Lucia crafted each and every one of her pieces herself.

Trying to lower her stress level, she clenched and unclenched her fingers. "I wish that was possible, Grandfather, but only I can finish crafting these particular pieces."

"Your mother and I will be very disappointed if you do not attend," Easton said with a sigh. "Charlotte has worked very hard to organize this. Your sisters and their husbands will be there, plus those members of my staff I previously mentioned.''

''Oh.'' From the time of night and her caller ID, she knew Easton was calling from her mother's penthouse. What members of the staff had he mentioned? Lucia paused. ''Did you say you were bringing other staff members besides Devon?''

''Of course I did,'' Easton replied. ''Ellie travels with me everywhere, and to make the numbers even, I will have Harrison escort her over from the embassy.''

Harrison would be there. That made all the difference in the world. At least she would see him again, stand in the same room as he. She could continue to try to show him that their relationship could be a wonderful, if temporary, experience for them both if he would only give in.

''I won't disappoint you.'' Or my mother, God forbid. Lucia remembered her manners. ''I'd be honored to come. I'm so glad you called me yourself.''

''Yes, well, I realized we haven't spent much time together, and I do want to get to know you. You remind me a lot of your father.''

''I do?'' Lucia was surprised.

''Yes. And believe me, despite what you may have heard about his wild youth, in the end, being like your father is a good thing.''

Lucia smiled, the compliment warming her. "Thank you."

"You're welcome. I'll send Devon for you tomorrow at five."

"Really, that's not necessary. I..."

Easton's tone indicated no arguments should be forthcoming. "I've already instructed Devon to pick you up tomorrow at five."

"Yes, Grandfather. I'll see you tomorrow."

Lucia set the receiver into its cradle and slumped back onto the sofa. Great. Another matchmaking attempt, and this time Easton was having Devon pick her up.

She bit her lip and then decided to look at the silver lining of the gray-cloud evening. Harrison would be there. At least she'd be able to see him again.

She wished he hadn't left. They needed to talk about Aspen. He would go, she was sure of it. If not, she'd just have to find a way to make it work to her advantage.

Harrison Montcalm was a man in desperate need of love, and Lucia knew that she was just the woman to provide it. Couldn't he sense how overflowing her heart could be?

She touched a finger to her lips. Perhaps he did. Perhaps that's why he'd run.

Even grown men still got scared, especially when faced with emotions they'd long denied.

Lucia picked herself up and went back to her workbench. She touched the tie tack she was making, the Korosolan symbol for honor.

She should have expected Harrison to flee. He was still thinking of his duty to the king, his duty to the throne.

He wasn't thinking of his duty to his heart.

Lucia began to work on the pin with an intensity reserved for pieces that really meant something to her.

She would convince Harrison he had a duty to his heart.

For his sake, she hoped he would accept.

"MISS CARRADIGNE?"

Lucia picked up the in-house phone so she could answer the doorman's buzz. "Yes, Frank?"

"A young gentleman named Sir Devon Montcalm is in the lobby."

There was no way she wanted to invite him up. "Tell him that I will be right down."

"Yes, ma'am."

Lucia set down the phone and smoothed out the dress she'd chosen. She perused her appearance one last time in the full-length mirror. She'd chosen a Ralph Lauren outfit consisting of a very simple black A-line sheath and a simple gray cashmere sweater.

Whereas everyone else would be dressed to the

nines, she wanted to be understated yet refined, like a cross between Audrey Hepburn and Jackie Kennedy Onassis.

She'd know if she had succeeded when she saw Harrison.

Lucia took the elevator down, and she saw Devon as soon as she rounded the corner into the lobby.

Two years her senior, Devon looked dashing in his uniform indicating his rank of captain of the Royal Guard. But in her eyes, no matter how good he looked, he didn't look half as wonderful as Harrison.

There were resemblances between father and son. Both had brown hair cut into a military style. Devon's was lighter than his father's, and didn't have the hints of gray at the temples. Devon stood two inches taller than his father, and had the same hazel-colored eyes.

Devon was in fantastic shape too, and his uniform only hinted teasingly at the wonderful body that lay underneath. What woman wouldn't find the younger Montcalm to die for?

Lucia, that was who.

She approached Devon, and much to her mortification, he bowed to her right there in the lobby.

Frank, the doorman, looked as if he would bust a gut. Somehow he managed to contain his surprise.

"Princess," Devon said.

"Not here," Lucia pleaded. Here she was Lucia Carradigne, not a princess. Her apartment was her last haven. She didn't want to lose that just yet. They walked to the curb in silence.

Unlike her mother who adored fur, Lucia preferred wool, and her long overcoat protected her from the slight evening chill. It had been a long winter across the United States, and New York City, despite being late April, hadn't seemed to warm up that much.

Devon opened the door to the Mercedes sedan and Lucia entered. Although she doubted he had any interest in her, he was loyal to his king, and Lucia wanted to make it extremely clear her stance on Easton's matchmaking. She sat herself on the opposite side of the back seat.

"Thank you for picking me up," she said as the driver pulled out into traffic.

"Anytime you require it, Princess, this sedan is at your disposal. It is equipped with all the latest security features."

How thrilling, Lucia thought.

Then she blurted, "I'm sorry. I don't mean to be rude. This is just awkward for me, and I'm not much into conversation."

"I understand," Devon replied.

"Thanks," Lucia said. Then she fell silent again. The remaining fifteen-minute drive she spent contemplating Harrison and his reaction last night.

She'd gone over it already a million times, so much that when Devon announced they'd arrived, she had to blink to come back to the present. She sighed, and let Devon help her from the car.

"Ah, there you are," King Easton said in greeting as Charlotte's butler, Quincy, ushered them into the Grand Room. Devon executed a perfect bow, and Lucia, her overcoat having been removed as she entered the apartment, made the appropriate curtsy.

Easton seemed to be in good spirits, and Lucia went forward and gave her grandfather a kiss on the cheek.

Her sisters then swarmed Lucia. CeCe looked radiant, her green eyes sparkling. Pregnancy obviously agreed with her, and Lucia told her that.

"It's wonderful," CeCe said, her chin-length strawberry blond hair pulled back tonight. She patted her stomach, which was getting bigger by the day. She looked over to where her husband, Shane, stood talking to Nicholas, Amelia's husband. "I never thought I would be this happy."

"Me neither," Amelia added, her gaze revealing the love she had for her husband. "Who would have thought that Mother would have been right? I always thought all she wanted was for us to be married. I love it."

Lucia pursed her lips as Quincy brought her a

glass of wine. "I still think I'll pass on believing Mother knows best."

"Not if she and Grandfather have their way," Amelia teased. "Hester told me she overheard them talking. I'm sure you've figured it out that they both think you and Devon would be perfect together."

"Uh-huh," Lucia mumbled incoherently. She turned her attention to the door. Harrison had arrived with Ellie.

A lump formed in her throat. He, like Devon, was dressed in full military uniform. His gaze caught hers from across the room, and Lucia noticed a slight smile in his eyes as he saw her.

Then the shutters came firmly down.

Lucia kept her sigh hidden. She instead listened to her sisters' conversations for a moment before making her excuses and heading to the kitchen.

"Sneaking out again," Hester chided Lucia as she strolled in.

Lucia gave her a kiss on her wrinkled cheek. "Had to come say hello to you."

Hester wiped her fingers on her apron. "I'd say it has more to do with a certain young man and your lack of interest in him."

"I don't want to appear rude. Am I that obvious?"

"Not to everyone else," Hester said, "but I know you and your reaction to your mother's constant and annoying matchmaking."

Lucia set her wineglass down and took a seat at the breakfast bar. "Devon doesn't do a thing for me," she admitted.

Hester paused for a moment from helping the Carradigne's cook, Bernice Styles, take out an appetizer tray. "But you've met someone who has," she said. "Remember? You told me about Harrison. Have you kissed him yet?"

Lucia's teeth toyed with her lips until Hester told her to stop.

"So you have," Hester said with a knowing nod. "And you can't have him, can you?"

"That's not the problem," Lucia said. She reached for a strand of her hair and jerked her hand down as Quincy strolled into the kitchen.

"What's not the problem?" he asked.

"You're the problem, old man," Hester said. She waved a finger at her beloved husband of over twenty-three years. "Get out there and do your job. No nipping at the cooking sherry for you tonight."

"Ah, you know me so well," Quincy said. He pulled at the starched collar of his butler uniform. "You know I hate this monkey suit."

"Yes, but I won't let you breathe sherry on the guests either."

"Make it up to me later?" Quincy said, a wicked gleam in his eye.

"Out," Hester ordered.

Lucia laughed aloud as she watched the

exchange. She'd often wondered, if her father had lived, if her own parents would be so open in their affection. Being only six when he'd died, she really couldn't remember.

"You know you're going to be missed if you don't get out there," Hester said. "Charlotte's been upstairs dressing for hours and she'll have your hide."

"My hide's gotten kind of tough where my mother is concerned," Lucia said. "Why do you think I moved out in the first place?"

"Because this apartment wasn't big enough for the both of ya," Hester said. "You were always fighting about something. Each of you just have different lifestyles, that's all."

"Maybe that's it," Lucia said.

Hester nodded. "But tonight isn't a night to worry about your mother. Now get out there and don't disappoint your grandfather. You can handle Sir Devon. Just show your grandfather a few flirtations. That'll really get him going."

Lucia shook her head. "I don't want to do that. Then Grandfather will want to continue with all this ridiculous matchmaking."

With the back of her hand Hester pushed her gray hair back off her forehead. "Haven't I taught you anything about men? I'm not talking about getting your *grandfather* going. It's the one you want to be with, Sir Harrison, who won't be able to handle seeing you flirting with his son.''

Lucia looked up at Hester in surprise. Hester had a knowing gleam in her eye. ''I know a bit about how to land a man and I know everything about you, Lucia my girl. Raised you like my own, I did.''

Lucia put her hand forward and covered Hester's. ''You did a good job.''

''Now get out there and wow him,'' Hester said. ''And just so you know, I think you've made a darn fine choice. Don't let anyone tell you otherwise.''

Chapter Seven

Harrison saw Lucia immediately as she slipped back into the crowd. While Easton may not have noticed the youngest Carradigne's disappearance, Harrison had.

"She's pretty, isn't she?" Ellie asked. She pressed her hands down, straightening the gray blazer that did absolutely nothing for her figure.

"She's a credit to her mother," Harrison replied, his gaze following Lucia as she went to speak to her sisters.

"Speaking of, where is Charlotte? Shouldn't she have been here before Easton?"

"Not tonight," Harrison said with a glance at his watch. A ding from the gallery told him that the private elevator had arrived from Charlotte's upper floor. "Tonight, being her house and her party, she can be fashionably late. Here she comes now."

"I hope I look like that at her age," Ellie breathed in awe as Charlotte arrived.

For Charlotte DeLacey Carradigne, at fifty, exemplified the epitome of youth. Her short, tousled hair was white, not gray, and it made her look beautiful and youthful.

Always put together in the latest designer couture, tonight Charlotte wore a fitted Vera Wang dress that set off her slim five-seven figure.

Charlotte curtsied to Easton, and then as Harrison watched, began making the rounds of greeting her married daughters, Lucia, Devon, and finally Harrison and Ellie.

"Sir Montcalm and Miss Standish," Charlotte said. Her perfume wafted to Harrison's nose, and while sensual and perfect for Charlotte, he found himself negatively comparing it to the pure scent that was Lucia.

"Duchess." Harrison greeted her with a low bow.

"Come, you must mingle. Miss Standish, you look wonderful tonight."

"Thank you, Duchess." Ellie curtsied.

And with that, Charlotte was off to take her position at Easton's side. Within minutes, Harrison noted, she and Easton had corralled Devon and Lucia together.

"Does she really mean for us to mingle?" Ellie asked.

"No," Harrison said.

"No?"

Harrison blinked. He'd spoken aloud his gut reaction to seeing Lucia and Devon together. He hadn't been answering Ellie. "Sorry. I thought you'd said something else. Of course she wants us to mingle. Feel free to talk to anyone here."

"Okay," Ellie said. "I just was checking the protocol, that was all. I haven't been having much fun this trip. Normally I get to actually go out and visit the countryside or something. I've been pretty much tied to the embassy, so I'd like to have some fun."

"Go socialize," Harrison told her. "It's okay." In reality, though, it wasn't.

He couldn't go mingle with Lucia. He didn't want to be here at all, except that Easton had insisted. "Your son will be there," he had said, "and I'm sure you'll want to see for yourself how well he and Lucia get along."

Actually, that was the whole reason Harrison didn't want to come. Just thinking about the situation was unbearable, and now to see the two of them so close together, talking and laughing and obviously having a good time, it was too much.

He could use air, but he'd already been a coward once. Escaping to the covered lanai off the Grand Room was not an option. Not tonight. Tonight he'd suffer through it, and somehow begin to close that part of his heart that Lucia had awakened with her kisses.

If the king had earmarked Devon to be prince consort to Lucia, then Harrison might as well get used to the horrible idea of being Lucia's father-in-law.

For once, doing his duty didn't feel right.

"Don't they make such a lovely couple?" Charlotte had approached Harrison. Harrison turned.

"Duchess," he acknowledged without giving her an answer.

"It will be the perfect move for your son," Charlotte said. "Prince consort of Korosol. Did you ever think you'd see one of your family marry royalty?"

"No," Harrison said honestly.

"I can't say I fault Easton in his choice," Charlotte said. "For years I've been trying to get Lucia settled with someone suitable, and now she's found Devon. You've done a fine job with him, Harrison, and I'll be delighted to join my family to yours."

"Thank you." Somehow Harrison managed to acknowledge what to him were cruel words. To Harrison's ears his tone sounded stiff, but Charlotte didn't seem to notice.

Instead, Quincy's opening of the door diverted her attention.

"Prince Markus Carradigne and Winston Rademacher," Quincy announced a moment later.

"Prince Markus." Charlotte moved to the entrance of the Grand Room. If she was put out by the intrusion of uninvited guests she didn't show it. "What a pleasant surprise!"

Markus accepted the kiss Charlotte gave him. "Oh, Charlotte, please accept my apology. I didn't know you were having a party."

"Nonsense. It's a gathering of family. You are most welcome." She gestured to the Grand Room. "I will be most offended if you don't stay."

"Really," Markus began, and Harrison had the distinct impression the prince and his trusted sidekick had been planning on crashing the Carradigne family party the whole time.

"Really," Charlotte said. "Your grandfather is here, and I know he hasn't seen as much of you as he would have liked. Come. Quincy, tell Hester to set two more plates."

"Yes, ma'am."

She led Markus to the Grand Room. "Look, girls, your cousin Markus is here."

It almost made Harrison ill to see even the polite, but stilted way the Carradigne women accepted Markus into their fold.

Harrison shook his head. They'd only known Markus in New York, not Korosol. Until now they'd never ever been a threat to his position, his desire for the throne. Even if they were a little suspicious, they would be polite and welcoming.

As if on autopilot, Harrison moved forward to

mingle. Despite his desire to stay away from Lucia, he wouldn't let her suffer at Markus's hands.

"You're looking even lovelier tonight, Lucia," Markus told his cousin.

"Thank you," Lucia said, stepping a bit back as if to widen her personal space.

"So, it must be love that's making you so radiant."

"Love?" Lucia gave Markus a quizzical look. "Why do you say that?"

"Ah, is it obvious to everyone but you? I'm talking about Sir Devon, of course. Everyone can tell how smitten he is with you."

"Oh, that," Lucia said. She wanted to roll her eyes at the absurdity of it all, but instead she smiled graciously. "I do believe that they are a little ahead of themselves. I have a trip to Aspen to make first."

"He would be a very lucky man," Markus said.

"Not you, too," Lucia said with a flat smile. She'd always liked Markus, until lately. Now there was an underlying something about him that set off her internal warning system. "I have enough on my mind besides worrying about finding a husband."

"Ah, yes." Markus nodded. "Has Easton asked you to be his heir?"

"Not yet," Lucia said. "And really, Markus, between you and me, I believe that is his personal business."

"Probably," Markus said with an eloquent shrug.

"Oh well," Lucia said with a smile that didn't quite reach her eyes. "I don't know when I'll be seeing you again. You would think that living in the same city we would see each other more often."

"Well, you will definitely be at the Inferno Ball, right?" Markus mentioned the high-society dance and charity auction being held in a few weeks' time.

"I wouldn't miss it," Lucia replied. "That's one of the events I actually love to attend."

"Then be sure to save me several dances."

"I can do that," Lucia said politely, her attention diverted as Harrison came into view.

He stepped forward right as a chiming of a bell interrupted Lucia and Markus's conversation.

"Dinner is served," Quincy announced.

OF COURSE Devon had been seated to Lucia's right, and King Easton to Lucia's left. Harrison didn't care about the king, but the fact that his son was sitting next to Lucia certainly bothered him.

Throughout the meal Harrison had found himself fuming from his place at the opposite end of the table. He'd had the perfect view of Lucia, but seeing his son paying attention to Lucia was not a view he wanted.

And as for dinner companions, he'd found himself flanked by Ellie on one side and Winston Rademacher on the other. One was more than acceptable, the other an absolute revulsion to be even in the same room with.

At least the food had been delicious.

He contemplated this, after dessert—a white-chocolate cake this time—when the group moved itself to the Grand Room.

During dinner he'd also had the opportunity to study his king. After all, Easton had been seated next to Lucia. But watching the king, Harrison's gut instinct had begun to trouble him. He found himself getting more and more worried about the monarch.

Ellie had told him that Easton had been appearing even more tired as of late. Even just this morning Harrison had seen it for himself, although tonight Easton had hidden exhaustion during dinner. But Harrison, after knowing the king for so long, had seen what was imperceptible to everyone else at the dinner table.

And it worried him. Because Easton felt time was short, Harrison had a feeling that his king was going to do something rash. Easton stood by the windows overlooking Central Park, and Harrison moved forward to stand by Easton's side.

"We do have to be leaving," Markus was telling his grandfather.

"I'm glad you came by," Easton said, and while

he sounded sincere, only Harrison sensed the underlying suspicion that laced the king's words.

"Leaving already?" Lucia approached the men.

"Yes," Markus said. "I have an early meeting tomorrow and I need my rest."

Right, Harrison thought. A one-on-one party with a liquor bottle was what really called Markus's name right now. Throughout the evening Quincy had politely held Markus to only two glasses of wine.

"Then perhaps I'll see you next at the ball," Lucia said. She accepted the kiss Markus bestowed on her cheek, and Harrison felt revulsion fill him. Markus should not defile Lucia's purity and goodness, even with a platonic kiss.

"At the ball," Markus repeated. "And good luck, Lucia, should you be appointed to the throne."

Lucia sent Markus a strange look and then shrugged noncommittally. "Good night then."

Markus bowed to his grandfather, and within moments, he and Winston had left the apartment.

Harrison felt the tension drain from his shoulders as soon as Markus's foul presence vanished from the apartment.

"So how are you, Harrison?"

He blinked and saw Lucia looking at him.

"I am well, thank you," he replied. "And you, Princess?"

Her eyes flinched as he used her title, but she quickly recovered. "Fine," Lucia said. Then, as if the moment had overwhelmed her, she opened her mouth to speak.

"Harrison," Easton interrupted his granddaughter. "Did you still need to speak with me?"

"Yes, sir," Harrison replied.

Easton nodded. He reached forward and patted Lucia gently on the arm. "We need to have a quick meeting. Would you excuse us?"

"Of course," Lucia said. While Easton missed it, Harrison could sense Lucia's frustration.

"We can use Charlotte's study," Easton said. Harrison followed him down the hall.

Easton sat in an overstuffed armchair. A gas fire flickered in the grate. "Tell me, Harrison, are our suspicions justified?"

"I think Markus is pure evil," Harrison put it bluntly. "But I have nothing to go on except my gut feeling."

"Gut feelings make or break rulers," Easton said. He closed his eyes. "My gut feeling tells me that Markus had something to do with his parents' deaths, just as Byrum and Sarah's friends suggested."

The room seemed to shrink. Whereas Harrison knew Easton had suspected that Markus wanted the throne badly, he didn't think Easton had truly believed the rumors that Markus arranged his parents' Jeep accident.

"You're silent, Harrison. Think I'm going crazy, do you?"

"No, sir," Harrison said. "I'm just contemplating the thought. There does seem to be something off about Markus. It'll be a minefield to deal with."

Easton opened his eyes. "I know. But I must take action."

"We'll step up your security, and that of your family, and…"

Easton waved a hand. "This rare disease will get me into the grave long before Markus ever can. That gives me a few years. Still, the truth of the matter is that I can't wait any longer to announce my heir."

"What do you mean?"

"I'm telling Lucia she's my heir."

Panic and shock filled Harrison. "When?"

"Tonight." Easton drummed his fingers on the upholstered arm of the chair. "I just wanted to tell you first. I want to make the announcement tomorrow."

"I haven't finished my investigation." Harrison prayed his desperation wasn't obvious. While he couldn't see Lucia ever again, especially not like last night in her apartment, he knew she needed a little more time. At least he wanted to be able to give her that.

Easton waved his hand again, as if brushing aside Harrison's protests. "Your investigation is finished. Don't worry about it. She's perfect for the role, and Devon will be a perfect mate for her. Will you please go bring her to me now?"

"Yes, sir," Harrison said. For in the end, he'd do his duty, just as he always did.

He strode through the Grand Room to where Lucia was speaking with her mother. From the sounds of the snippets he overheard, her mother wasn't pleased with the simplicity of Lucia's clothing. He frowned. Why wasn't Charlotte satisfied? Couldn't she see how lovely her daughter was? She'd outshone everyone tonight.

"Pardon me," Harrison intruded. "King Easton requests that Princess Lucia join him immediately in the study."

"Oh," Charlotte said, and Harrison knew Charlotte was already envisioning what Easton wanted to say.

Lucia frowned, and Harrison's heart broke at seeing her stubborn expression. "If you would please follow me."

As they stepped out of the Grand Room, Lucia turned to him. "So do you plan on ignoring me all night?"

"I'm not ignoring you," he replied, knowing that the words he spoke were lies. He'd become quite the falsehood spreader lately, which didn't sit well with his code of honor. "I'm simply doing my job."

As he suspected, Lucia didn't dignify him with a response. After all, what was there to say? He'd just told her what he'd chosen.

And, as at the wedding reception, it wasn't her.

As he opened the door, he wished he could tell her he hated himself for it, that he wished it could be different.

But those words, he knew, would only complicate matters.

Lucia was the next queen of Korosol.

He was adviser to the king.

Never the twain shall meet.

"Lucia, come in," Easton called. He looked up at Harrison. "Harrison, in about five minutes, will you please bring me some ice water?"

"Of course," Harrison replied.

And with that, he closed the door behind him, shutting Lucia in with her future, a future with him left standing on the outside.

Chapter Eight

"Yes, Grandfather?" Lucia entered Charlotte's study and perched on the edge of a leather settee. She'd never liked Charlotte's study much. It had always been too dark, too perfect. Lucia loved bright open spaces, and even though the study had a nice view of Columbus Avenue, Lucia didn't like the room.

Maybe it reminded her of how her mother had carved out a business empire at the expense of being a mother to her daughters.

It had been Hester who had taken Lucia to dance lessons, not Charlotte.

"Lucia, we need to have a serious talk," Easton said.

Lucia cocked her head slightly, and waited for him to continue.

"I have decided to name you my heir."

Even though she'd suspected the announcement,

and she had known it was coming, Lucia inwardly reeled. She'd thought she had more time.

Hadn't Harrison gotten her a week?

"I'm surprised," she managed to say finally.

"Surely not," Easton said. His eyes narrowed slightly "You knew Harrison thoroughly investigated your background."

"Yes, but I didn't think he was finished," she said. "He told me he had more to do."

"He wasn't finished," Easton admitted. "But I've seen and heard enough to make my decision without the rest. You are perfect and will make a lovely queen."

"Thank you, I think," Lucia said. Reverting to another age-old habit, she pulled on a tendril of her hair.

"You think?" Easton seemed highly perturbed at her lack of enthusiasm.

"It's just so sudden," Lucia said hastily. She tried to regroup.

She could see her mother's reaction as if Charlotte was listening at the keyhole right now. Her mother would be having a fit.

"I'm sorry not to sound more grateful. Believe me, I am," Lucia said quickly. "I'm just surprised, that's all. I thought you weren't going to make the announcement quite so fast. I thought you were going to wait for a little while longer."

"Circumstances dictate that the announcement

be made as soon as possible. You are willing to be my heir, yes?'' Her grandfather's gaze bored into hers and Lucia shifted uncomfortably.

"Er, yes,'' Lucia said. Did she have a choice? Unlike CeCe, she wasn't pregnant, and unlike Amelia, she wasn't secretly married. And her mother would wring her neck if she blew this opportunity.

Lucia straightened. She'd never really had a choice when she'd been born. She was a Carradigne, and the family responsibilities she'd been studiously avoiding for so long had just reached out to hook her and pull her back in.

She couldn't disappoint her grandfather. He believed in her; he believed enough to name her queen.

"Yes, I will be queen,'' she said. "But there is a small catch.''

Easton's joy at her announcement wavered slightly. "A catch?''

"I have loose ends to tie up. I have a jewelry show in Aspen. I told you about that. I'd like you to wait to make the announcement until I return from my trip to Colorado.''

The king tapped his fingers on the arm of the chair. "I can do that,'' he said. "When exactly will you be returning?''

"Let's see. Tonight is Sunday. I leave Tuesday and return Sunday. I need one week. You could make the announcement next Monday.''

Easton's expression showed his contemplation. Seconds passed slowly, and Lucia heard each tick as the grandfather clock counted them off.

"One week," he agreed. At that moment Harrison reentered the room carrying a pitcher of water and two glasses.

"Put them on the table and sit down," Easton commanded. Harrison complied and Easton filled his adviser in. "Lucia has agreed to be queen."

"That's good," Harrison said, although deep down he knew that this time what was good for Korosol was bad for him.

"She also has told me about some loose ends, as she calls them, she needs to tie up. Something about a trip to Aspen. I'd like you to send Devon with her."

"No," both Lucia and Harrison said at the same time. Easton looked back and forth between them.

"Grandfather," Lucia said with a warning glance at Harrison, "that would look inappropriate. Everyone knows how much you want Devon and I to, well, to be blunt, fall in love and get married. Just think of the press if Krissy Katwell got a hold of the fact that we went to Aspen together."

"That's what I was thinking," Harrison added. "Devon can call Alexandra Metzler over from Korosol. She's a top-notch member of the Royal Guard and she'd be a good escort for Lucia."

"Oh, that's not necessary," Lucia said hastily.

"I wouldn't want her to travel all the way from Korosol on such short notice."

"I'm not allowing you to go by yourself," Easton said. He stared at her, as if daring her to defy that logic.

"Of course not," Lucia said. She turned a smile on Harrison. "Harrison could accompany me. After all, he *is* going to be my father-in-law."

In his seat she saw Harrison squirm. Too bad, Lucia thought. She wasn't going to let him wiggle out of this. They had one week, and she wanted every minute of it. "Separate rooms, of course," Lucia told her grandfather sincerely, although she knew the hotel was booked solid and probably wouldn't be able to accommodate the late request.

"Agreed," Easton said. His tone said that the decision was now set in stone.

"Thank you," Lucia said. She rose and threw her arms around Easton's neck.

"You're welcome," Easton said gruffly, and with that, Lucia straightened.

A knock on the door interrupted the meeting and Harrison rose to admit Devon. "I've just been paged," he said without preamble, "and I have news."

"You may go," Easton told Lucia. "Good night, Lucia."

"Good night, Grandfather. Devon, if it's all

right, I'm leaving now. The driver will take me back."

Seeing the king's approval, Devon said, "Certainly, Princess." He bowed.

As she left the room, she contemplated Devon's news.

Whatever it was, it must be big. For once, Easton had dropped his matchmaking plans in favor of it.

Lucia shrugged and made her way back to the Grand Room to say her goodbyes. For one week, Korosol and the business of running it was going to be the furthest thing from her mind.

She had a man's heart to free.

"So, TELL ME," King Easton said, "who is behind the press articles?"

Devon shifted in his seat, and to hear him better, Harrison leaned forward. Whoever the source was, he or she had defiled Lucia, and that was unacceptable.

"Rademacher," Devon said. Harrison felt a bitterness immediately fill him.

"Winston?" King Easton reeled as if he'd been delivered a physical blow. "You're saying Winston Rademacher is Krissy Katwell's source?"

"Yes," Devon confirmed with a nod. "We've managed to track down several phone calls from Rademacher to Katwell and vice versa. I also have witnesses who have seen the two of them together several times.''

''That's not conclusive evidence,'' Harrison pointed out.

''I know,'' Devon said, ''but right now it's the best we've got. We aren't able to locate anyone else who has an interest in exposing the secrets of your granddaughters, Your Highness. We've tracked down the vendetta angle, but it's a dead end.''

Easton leaned forward, his gaze connecting with Harrison's. Based on what they had discussed earlier, Harrison knew exactly what Easton was thinking.

If Winston was the source, then Markus was behind the actions. It meant Markus would stoop low to discredit his cousins in the eyes of their grandfather and the world.

That in turn made Easton's suspicions of Markus's involvement in the deaths of his parents much more realistic.

Easton seemed to age right before Harrison's eyes, and Harrison's heart empathized with his friend and beloved king.

He couldn't imagine a worse situation to be in.

''You will tell me when you have full confirmation,'' Easton finally said.

''Of course,'' Devon replied. ''I hope to have more solid proof soon, but I wanted you to know as soon as I had anything.''

"Good work," Easton said. He leaned back and stared off into space for a moment. Finally his attention returned to the men in the room. "So, Devon, describe my granddaughter to me."

"Which one?" Devon said, and for an instant Harrison felt sorry for him.

"My youngest, Lucia."

"She's lovely," Devon replied, and Harrison heard the honesty in his son's voice. A pang of jealousy shot through him despite Devon's noncommittal answer. "I'm enjoying getting to know her."

"Good," Easton said. "I want you to spend a lot more time with her when she returns from Aspen next Sunday. I told her tonight that I've named her my heir."

"That's wonderful news, Your Grace," Devon said. "I know you've wanted to wrap this up."

"The announcement won't be until next Monday. Harrison will fill you in on all the details. But after the announcement, I want you constantly at Lucia's side. You will be her personal bodyguard and adviser."

"I would be honored," Devon agreed, and Harrison's jealousy raged as he saw his son's excitement at the prospect.

"Excellent. I'll leave you to discuss it with your father." And with that, Easton rose slowly and exited the room.

"Harrison, did you know about this?" Devon's excitement invaded the room as he dropped his reserve the moment Easton left. "What an honor!"

Harrison managed a smile. Why shouldn't Devon be excited, Harrison thought. His son had just been handed the responsibility of being the adviser to the heir of the Korosolan throne. Out with the old, in with the young.

Harrison mentally berated himself. By the rood, he was jealous! Extremely jealous!

No matter what, he shouldn't be jealous. He couldn't have these possessive feelings for Lucia. Those feelings were off-limits.

Easton had earmarked her for Devon, and now the king had planted the seeds for the eventual fruition of the relationship.

For the first time in his life, Harrison knew true hurt.

"You're quiet," Devon observed. His face sobered for a moment. "Oh, I didn't think. This means that you're out of a job."

"No, I'll still be Easton's adviser as long as he needs me."

"But you've always advised the throne," Devon said.

His son's look pained Harrison. How could he do this to Devon? No, Harrison knew he had to let his son have his moment, his future. If only that future didn't involve Lucia!

"It's time for the next generation," Harrison replied, knowing that no matter how hard the words were to say, he must say them and reassure Devon. Worse, Harrison knew he must do as his code of honor dictated.

Deep down, he knew the words he had just spoken were true. It was time for the next generation; he just didn't like it much.

In the height of Devon's moment, he had to admit the worst fact of his life. He was jealous of his own son.

The reason was Lucia. How could she not fall in love with someone as young, energetic and attractive as his son, Devon?

Harrison knew that by working closely with him on matters of Korosol, Lucia and Devon would become extremely close. Their mutual interest in the country would draw them together. Even if they didn't love each other now, they would form a pleasant companionship that would serve them well into the future.

"It's a great opportunity for you," he finally told his son. "I'm proud of the work you've done."

"Thanks," Devon said, his elation sobering again. "I still have more to do."

"You'll finish it," Harrison said, for he knew his son was a by-the-book man who would accomplish everything he set his mind to.

"Hopefully in time," Devon said. "So, while we

have a few moments, do you want to fill me in on Lucia's trip to Aspen?''

Aspen.

Harrison wanted to close his eyes.

Even hearing the word was like nails to a coffin. Lucia had insisted that he accompany her to Aspen, and Easton had agreed. Torture would have been a better alternative.

''Let's meet tomorrow and I'll give you the details then,'' he said. ''I'm tired, and I'm going to see if Ellie is ready to return to the embassy.''

''I'll take her,'' Devon offered.

''Thank you.'' Harrison stood up. ''I'll see you, say, about ten tomorrow?''

''Yes,'' Devon replied as he stood. ''Have a good night, Harrison.''

''You too.'' Harrison walked to the Grand Room and quickly said his goodbyes.

A few minutes later he leaned back against the mirrored elevator wall as the elevator descended toward the lobby of Charlotte's building.

Easton was right. Lucia needed someone younger, someone invigorating. He was too old, too outdated. Like Easton, his time in the sun was drawing to a close. It was time to let his son shine.

And doing that meant staying as far away from Lucia Carradigne as possible. He could do it, but it would be a test of his mettle.

Harrison reminded himself that he was made of strong, sturdy stuff.

He could keep his hands off Lucia and his feelings in check for one last week.

He'd do it if it killed him.

As he stepped into an embassy car, he realized that it just might.

Chapter Nine

A few days later, going to Aspen wasn't killing him. He was enjoying it too much, even though he knew he shouldn't.

Indeed, it had been a wonderful flight.

Harrison studied the woman sitting next to him in the chauffeured car heading west on Interstate 70. As soon as Lucia and he had taken their first-class seats on the plane, all his resolve to stay as far away from her as possible had vanished.

He couldn't help himself.

Already he'd failed in his objective, which was to stay neutral and not emotionally involved with Lucia. She'd talked the whole flight, and it would have been rude not to respond, right? So they'd conversed the entire flight from New York to Denver, where they'd picked up a hired car.

"I hate flying into Aspen," Lucia had told him when he'd asked why they didn't fly straight in. "I don't like small planes. I call them puddle jumpers, and while everyone says they're safe, I have visions of being smashed into the side of a mountain.''

And that had gotten them talking about Harrison's past, and how he had learned to fly. He'd shared many of his stories with her, including the one of how he'd saved Easton's life by diving in front of an assassin's bullet.

He brought his attention back to the present.

''You'll love this place,'' Lucia was saying as the car began the climb into the mountains surrounding Denver. ''I've been staying here ever since I discovered it a few years back. We'll be able to ski right out the door and onto the slopes.''

''It sounds wonderful,'' he said, although the thought of even being in the same hotel with Lucia was extremely unsettling.

''Oh, it is. It's one of the smaller hotels in the area. I like it because it's private and quiet.''

A few hours later, as the car pulled into the driveway of the Victorian inn, Harrison could see why Lucia loved it. A storybook princess needed a storybook hotel, and that's exactly what it was.

From his vantage point, the gables of the roofline almost seemed to be minimountains themselves. The inn blended into the surroundings instead of appearing like a cookie-cutter image thrust out of time and space.

The bellhop came around to open the car door,

and a breath of cool mountain air hit them as they stepped out. Lucia turned her face toward it.

She inhaled deeply, and Harrison found himself caught up in her enthusiasm.

"Freedom," she said as they went through the oversize oak doors. "I love being in the mountains. It's so freeing."

Harrison could only manage to nod. Seeing Lucia like that, framed against the setting sun and the mountains, he wanted her like no other.

"Do you have any other bags?"

"No," Lucia said to the bellhop. Using an insured carrier, she had already shipped her jewelry to the art gallery. She turned and entered the inn.

Within moments she'd registered. "Suite 25," she told the bellhop.

"Very good, ma'am." He began to carry their luggage away.

"Wait," Harrison said. The man stopped and Harrison turned to Lucia. "One room?"

"That's all they had," she answered. He saw her jaw tilt, meaning her stubbornness was in full force. She waved the bellhop on and he vanished.

"Did you change the reservation?"

"Of course I did." Her green eyes blazed angrily. "They said they would accommodate me if they could. Obviously they couldn't. It's a small inn and always at capacity."

"We were supposed to have two rooms," he

said, his panic at having to stay in a room with Lucia mounting. He already wanted her, how was he to resist if they were together in the same room?

Harrison counted to ten, something he hadn't had to do since childhood. "I'll need to stay somewhere else. I'll go—"

Lucia put her hands on her hips and interrupted him. "You will do no such thing, and we will certainly not discuss this right here."

She was right, and Harrison calmed himself. They could have a civilized discussion up in her hotel suite. He just wished he didn't feel so set up.

He told her so the moment they walked into the room.

"You set this up."

Lucia didn't even bother to feign indignation or ignorance. "I did call the inn. If they could have accommodated us separately they would have. Instead, this suite is perfectly acceptable."

More so, if one counted on suite seduction. He had to somehow regain control of the situation. "It is nice," he said carefully.

"Nice?" Lucia's disbelief echoed in the high-ceilinged room. "You call a king-size four-poster bed, a fireplace and Victorian-brocade drapes nice?"

"It's, well, romantic," Harrison said.

"It's supposed to be," Lucia said. "That's why I stay here. That's what this inn is all about."

"Well, we're not supposed to be romantic," Harrison told her. "You're royalty. I'm your, your bodyguard, for lack of a better term."

"I do not need a bodyguard," Lucia asserted. Fire danced in her green eyes. "I can handle myself, and I have for years before you walked into my life."

"Your grandfather appointed me—"

She cut him off sharply. "My grandfather is not here!"

"No, he's not, but I have a duty…"

Her chin thrust forward. "You have no duty to me. You're relieved of it. Finished. You're on vacation. I order you to have fun and relax. Goodness knows you need it."

He did, but Harrison's pride wouldn't let him. He had to make Lucia see that whatever fantasy she'd created in her head, it couldn't be reality.

He tossed his briefcase on the sofa. "I'll sleep over here."

"You are being absolutely ridiculous," Lucia said. Her temper flared. "You're too tall. Take the bed. I'll take the sofa. I'm sure it folds out somehow."

"Lucia, please," he protested. "I don't mean to offend you, but this can't happen."

"What can't happen?" Her tone told him her anger had not yet peaked. He gestured around the suite.

"This. Us."

She didn't bother to try to deny what she wanted. "Why? What is so wrong?"

"I work for your grandfather."

"So?"

Harrison tried another tactic to make her understand. "I'm too old for you."

"You're only as old as you feel, and right now I'm tired of this conversation," Lucia retorted. "I've made it perfectly clear how I feel about you. If you want me, I'll be downstairs in the lounge."

And with that, Lucia stormed out the door and slammed it behind her.

Harrison stared at the closed door. He headed for the door, determined to go after her. He couldn't go after her. She wasn't his to have. He had to let her go. With a sigh, he sat down on the sofa to wait.

LUCIA LEANED against the closed suite door and took a deep breath. She'd acted impulsively, and she didn't want to live to regret it.

As soon as she stepped into the hallway her instinct hit her with the truth. He wouldn't come after her. She knew that he had too much pride, too much belief that he was doing the right thing by staying away from her.

Time to retrench and try another tactic.

She inserted her key into the door and opened it.

From the doorway she could see Harrison, staring off into space. Her heart broke.

"I'm sorry," she said.

He looked up, his face haggard.

"I should have respected you more. I won't put any further pressure on you by telling you that I want you. Could we just manage to be friends for the rest of this trip and have fun? It's my last week of being a normal everyday person, and I'd really like to just be free for one last time. Let's not ruin it for either of us. All right?"

Harrison nodded. "That would be fine," he said.

Lucia smiled. "Thank you."

He stood and straightened. "No, thank *you*. Please understand, Lucia, it's not that I don't want you. I do. But it can't happen."

"I know," she said, crossing her fingers behind her back so the lie didn't count. She hoped the childish gesture brought her luck. She was going to need it. "I'll respect your space."

Harrison rubbed the back of his neck with his hand. "So we'll be friends."

"Friends," Lucia agreed. She stepped forward. "How about I call room service and have them send something up?"

"That sounds great." He still looked suspicious, as if she had something up her sleeve.

"Dinner then," Lucia said. She smiled as she retrieved the menu from its holder. Go ahead and feel safe, Harrison, she mentally told him. I know you care for me, and you will be mine before this weekend is over. Just you wait and see.

LUCIA CONTEMPLATED her vow late the next morning as she and Harrison headed toward the ski lifts. They'd gotten a late start, two hours later than originally planned. But that was to be expected.

They'd slept in.

Not together, however. She'd insisted Harrison take the bed and she'd taken the foldout sofa.

It was a move that had the results she'd wanted. As he had on the airplane flight, Harrison was finally again loosening up. Last night had helped. Dinner had been delicious, and after studiously avoiding the specific topic of them, they'd talked about anything and everything until about one in the morning.

They'd laughed and shared, and Lucia knew deep in her soul that they'd grown closer despite all of Harrison's reservations to the contrary.

She would win him. He needed love, her love. It was only a matter of time as to when he would accept the gift she offered him.

"Shall we start slow to warm up?" Harrison asked.

"Certainly," she answered. "Green bunny slopes it is."

Hours later, Lucia and Harrison had worked their

way up from green easier slopes to blue moderate to black diamonds—the difficult slopes. He was an excellent skier, and she'd loved skiing with someone who could keep up with her. "What do you think?" she asked. "Shall we try to do one of the double black diamonds now?"

"Absolutely," Harrison said. He lifted his goggles so he could look at her. "It's getting late, so we'll make it the last run of the day."

"Sounds great," she said. She lifted her poles. "Let's go."

And off they went.

"You know," Lucia told him on the ski lift, "when I first started skiing I couldn't get off the lift right. I could ski a blue, but I couldn't manage to just glide off the lift and come to a stop. I fell each time. It was quite mortifying."

She shifted her legs and stared straight out. "I also really don't like these things much."

"They are a bit unnerving," Harrison admitted. "You have more of a guard on a roller coaster or Ferris wheel."

"True," she said as they reached the spot where it was time to get off their chair. "Here we go."

"Perfect," Harrison said as he met her at the end of the tiny mound.

"It took years of practice," she admitted. "Come on."

Harrison followed Lucia toward the double black

diamond slope. He had to admit, once Lucia had stopped pressuring him, he'd been having the time of his life.

Flying down the slopes, jumping moguls with her at his side, Harrison had never felt more alive or freer.

Lucia was a breath of fresh air. She was freedom itself.

"Watch that patch!" she called, but it was too late. Harrison felt the skis slip and heard the grating sound as the runners hit the ice. He managed to make the correction, but still found himself sliding down part of the slope on the back of his ski pants.

"Are you okay?" she said as she quickly came to a stop beside him.

"Yes. Only my pride is bruised," he replied with a wry laugh.

"That's why these are double blacks," she said, glad that he was okay. A fall could be dangerous no matter how good a skier someone was.

"Hey, folks." A ski patrolman came over to them. "Do you know of any other skiers either in front or behind you?"

"No." Lucia shook her head. Harrison stood and brushed the white powder off his ski pants. Then he clipped his boot back onto his ski.

"Okay. Be careful and let the woman at the end know when you get off the slope. We're closing this slope behind you because it's getting too icy."

"Now he tells us," Harrison joked after the man skied on ahead.

"Well, let's finish this and then go get some dinner. That should warm us up," Lucia said.

Harrison watched her lead off. She hadn't laughed; she hadn't even been morbidly concerned to the point of being annoying. She'd just been, well, perfect. She'd handled the situation of his fall perfectly.

Harrison mulled that over as the wind brushed his cheek. Lucia fit a hole in his life he hadn't known existed until he met her.

She fit him.

They were reaching the end of the slope, and with a push of determination, Harrison passed her and beat her to the bottom. He stopped and removed his goggles so he could watch Lucia come down. She was laughing.

Then he realized why. As she approached him she turned sharply, dug her skies in and sprayed him with a wave of fresh powder.

"Hey!" He tried to use his sleeve to brush the snow off, but she'd covered his ski parka, too. Getting rid of the snow was absolutely useless, and without even thinking, Harrison simply let his emotions reign.

He grabbed a handful of white powder and tossed it over her head.

"So you're going to play that way!" Lucia

pushed her goggles up and grabbed a handful of white powder.

Within moments, they'd started an all-out snow fight. "No you don't!" Lucia suddenly called, and she grabbed at his sleeve before he could dump the next handful of snow over her.

Knocked off balance, Harrison found his skis once again flying out from under him. This time he and Lucia both fell down into the soft powder.

Lucia rolled, still trying to put snow down his back. He grabbed both of her hands and held them out at her sides. "Now what are you going to do?" he teased. His face was mere inches from hers.

"This," she said, and, wiggling free, she threaded her hands behind his head.

Harrison gazed down at her, the invitation obvious. All he had to do was…he lowered his lips and the magic began.

There in the snow, heaven again descended. No choir of angels could have had a sweeter song than was found in Lucia's kiss. He teased the roof of her mouth, and deepened the spiraling kiss.

To Lucia, finally having Harrison kiss her was wonderful. There, cradled in the snow, she felt the opposition—the coldness at her back and the warmness at her front. The combination excited and fueled her. He was kissing her, really kissing her.

Finally.

"I want you," he admitted to her as he pulled his lips away. "But not here."

She blinked. "Snow," she said, a silly grin covering her face.

"Exactly. And that woman coming to see if we're okay probably wouldn't want to be a witness."

"No," Lucia said with a shake of her head. After Harrison stood, she righted herself. Somehow she'd lost her hat as well.

"You're the last ones off the slope, right?"

"Right," Harrison said.

"Great," the woman said. "I thought I saw someone else over here a minute ago, but I might have been wrong. Either that or he must have left."

"Time to go," Harrison told Lucia as the woman moved away.

"Harrison." Lucia suddenly felt desperation. They'd come so close and she didn't want to slide back now. She reached forward and touched her glove to his sleeve. "Take me to the hotel room."

She saw a flicker of hesitation. "We don't even have a full week, Lucia," he said. "You aren't a one-night, much more a two-night type of woman. You need commitment, something I can't give you."

"I don't care," Lucia said, and in her heart she knew that no truer words had been spoken. "I have only this week before I'm married to Korosol and all it embodies. For the rest of this week, this one week, Harrison—'' her voice cracked ''—I want you.''

He felt horribly torn in half. How he wanted to say yes, and how he knew he shouldn't. ''It's improper, Lucia. I'm too old, and your life is already going to be complicated enough. We can't do this. I can't add another complication.''

Lucia straightened. Her chin jutting forward, she prepared herself for the battle of winning his heart.

This time she would argue right back. Now it was time to fight, and he would cave if given the right argument. She knew his heart was ready; it just had to be freed.

''Look, Harrison, for this last week I want to live my life my way. Next week I'll be named queen, and I'll give up everything I've ever cared about. Let me have this last memory. I want you, don't deny me that.''

Harrison sighed, his resistance weakening. He tried one last argument in order to make her see reason. ''What about Devon? Easton wants you to marry Devon. How can I make love to you when you're to marry my son?''

Uncaring of the cold air, Lucia pulled off her glove. She reached forward and touched Harrison's cheek, her fingers immediately warming his skin.

''I've never wanted Devon,'' she said. Her voice radiated her sincerity. ''I've wanted you from the moment I first saw you.''

Chapter Ten

There, at the base of the mountain, time stood still as Lucia's admission shattered him. Harrison reached forward and drew her to him. He had to kiss her, and he had to kiss her now.

His lips touched hers, and he felt the tremors begin to travel through his body.

"We need to go," he whispered, his meaning clear.

Her green eyes gazed at him. "Yes," she said, still knowing she had work to do. "We need to go."

Tenderly Lucia reached forward, lowered his lips to hers one more time. Lucia's kiss was soft, gentle, and he explored her sweet mouth tenderly, as if she were fragile, priceless glass.

He let her lead, let her initiate the bolder and bolder strokes of their mating mouths until finally he couldn't bear it anymore.

"Lucia." He groaned out her name, passionately rolling it off his tongue. "Lucia."

"It's okay, Harrison," she whispered back. "Give in, darling. Remember, I want you just as much. Tonight, this week, is for us."

With her words Harrison finally caved. She smiled at him, her face radiant. "Now we can go."

Harrison thanked the gods as he and Lucia skied back to the inn.

TWILIGHT FILTERED IN the partially open blinds as Harrison gently laid her down on the huge four-poster bed, kissing her all the while.

He was so strong, yet so tender, Lucia mused as his fingers fumbled at her shirt buttons. This was her hero, the man she loved. She'd never felt freer, more in heaven, more in love.

She'd been made for this, made for him, she thought as she ran her fingers over his shirt. Already this moment was different from their previous encounter that her grandfather had interrupted.

Yes, tonight she wanted more. She wanted no distractions, no doubts and no interruptions. She wanted his passion, his all.

She let her hands grow bold, running them over his torso and underneath his shirt. His chest was fit, toned, strong. As Lucia touched him, skin warmed skin. With a groan of desire, his hands cupped her breasts. She quivered, and he freed them from her bra.

His mouth suckled and lathed her nipples and she cried out with the rapture of the sensations. As his lips moved over her body Lucia spiraled out of control. No one had ever touched her like this before, or made her feel so wondrously special.

Her limbs loosened, and then tightened with the sensations he sent coursing through her. When his lips came back to recapture hers, Lucia grew even bolder.

She wanted what had been denied to her when Easton had phoned. She wanted what she was meant for since the beginning of time.

She kissed him. His eyebrows. His ears. His cheekbones. His neck. She planted kisses on his chest, his stomach.

In the last vestiges of the day, their clothes disappeared and their bodies melted and molded together. He touched her, tasted her and possessed her.

Lucia shuddered from the joy of it. Her body wanted and craved the welcome invasion that would soon make her whole.

When it finally came she was more than ready. Finally he prepared himself and boldly made Lucia complete. As he filled her, Harrison brought her to heights never imagined in her wildest fantasies, and then some.

He stilled for a moment, reveling in the feeling of two becoming one. Lucia shuddered as she writhed in delighted ecstasy.

She tightened her grip on his back as he called her name once. His hips began to undulate, thrusting gently at first, then bolder, harder, until Lucia was right there on the amazing journey with him.

She peaked first, then with him, and then she crested again and again as he carried her over the edge to where time seems to stop and nothing matters but the merging of two souls long destined to become one.

He held her tightly afterward, pulling her closer until her head snuggled against his firm naked chest. Lucia allowed herself to relax.

She wasn't sure how long she slept before she found herself waking up. He was stroking her cheek with his finger and she found herself looking deeply into his hazel eyes.

Their lovemaking began again with a fervor equaling, then surpassing, the time before.

So this is what true love was all about, Lucia thought, delighting in the fact that Harrison was stroking her hair. Never after lovemaking had she ever felt so complete, so whole.

"You're quiet," Harrison whispered, his breath warm on her cheek.

"I was just thinking," she replied as she began to drift into another contented sleep. She felt the mattress give as Harrison raised himself onto his elbow. He traced her cheek with the back of his forefinger.

"Penny for those thoughts then," he said. "Share them with me, sleepyhead."

The sun had fully set, and the room had drifted into a pale darkness. Harrison's face was in the shadows, and Lucia closed her eyes.

Sleep tiptoed on little cat feet to claim her, and delightedly her body surrendered to the contented rest it needed. She could continue to feel him gently stroke her cheek.

Was he waiting for her answer still? She couldn't tell him the truth. Not yet. Not when he didn't love her back. She couldn't say those words and put that type of pressure on him.

She simply had to take what he could offer her, for something was better than nothing.

Besides, she didn't want Harrison to stay with her out of duty, out of a respect for feelings he didn't have for her.

No, for this week he was free, just as she was. Here in Aspen the real world didn't exist. All that existed was simply the love they could share for just this one brief moment of time.

"Phenomenal," she murmured, and then the blissful aftermath of sleep swept her away to the place where dreams came true.

Harrison stared down at her face. Never had he

seen a face so angelic in slumber. He pushed all the remaining doubts out of his head. Making love with Lucia had been more than phenomenal. It had been heaven, and already he wanted more. For just this week, he'd follow her lead and her advice. He'd let himself be free. He kissed her forehead once. "Thank you, sweetheart."

She mumbled something before shifting and falling even deeper into sleep.

"Me too," he replied.

"SO, WHAT'S ON tomorrow's agenda?" Harrison asked later as they soaked in the oversize claw-foot tub somewhere around midnight.

Lucia drew a soapy hand over Harrison's back. She pressed him back into her chest and nibbled on his ear. "Tomorrow's agenda is skiing in the morning. Then we have the cocktail party celebrating the opening of my show later in the evening."

"Anything else?"

"Of course," she said as she began to massage his broad shoulders. "Dinner by the fireplace, more baths and definitely staying in bed late."

"Sleeping late, huh?"

"Who said anything about sleeping?" Lucia teased. She blew lightly in his ear, and underneath the warm, foamy water Harrison felt himself stir.

He was ready for her again. He'd never experienced such a fast recovery, or desire, for a woman in his life. "I've noticed you sleep in spurts."

"I do," Lucia said. "I've learned to survive on little sleep. When an idea hits me in the middle of the night, I just get up and go with it."

Her hand moved around his chest to caress his nipples. He shifted, pressing himself back even farther against her.

"Feel good?" she asked.

"Excellent," he admitted as her hands roamed over the lumpy scar from where he'd taken the bullet meant for Easton. Her hands traveled even lower, and he groaned aloud as she found the part of him now throbbing.

"You make me feel good too," she said, her hands stroking his flesh. "I've never felt this way with anyone else."

With a groan, he surrendered to her ministrations and the wonderment of her magical hands.

They never made it skiing the next morning.

Lucia smiled at the memory of her and Harrison's lovemaking. Instead of skiing, he'd lit a fire in the fireplace. They had shared an early breakfast, followed by more lovemaking. Then while Aspen received fresh snow, they had slept most of the afternoon away.

"Your jewelry is lovely," a woman said, her voice bringing Lucia's attention back into the present.

"Thank you," Lucia said. She was at her show, and she took a sip of bubbly champagne. She and Harrison had been mingling with the jet-set crowd partying at the art gallery for most of the evening.

Pam, the gallery owner, approached. "Absolutely a success, Lucia," she said. "Julia bought three of your pieces. She's going to have a dress designed especially to complement the gold necklace."

Lucia smiled. As a Carradigne she didn't really need the income from the sale of the pieces. The joy of selling them was what was most important. Plus, Pam had just made a hefty commission, and Lucia knew her friend could use the financial boost. While her gallery was a success, Pam was in the middle of a nasty divorce.

"I'm glad it's been a good opening," Lucia said. "I probably won't be able to have another show for a while." Probably never, but Lucia didn't feel like thinking about that right now.

"I'd say not," Pam said with a knowing gleam in her eye. "I'd hide out all day in my apartment if I had a man like that to keep me company."

Lucia followed Pam's gaze. Harrison had proven most adept at mingling with the diverse crowd. Of course, recent rich divorcées had made a beeline for the distinguished, sexy gentleman in the tuxedo, but Lucia hadn't minded. She'd dismissed the pangs of jealousy. For this week he was hers, and she was secure in that knowledge.

Besides, Harrison had stood by her side as often as necessary, as if knowing when she'd needed him there. He'd even known when to move away, when she'd needed to just be alone with the people enjoying her work.

He sensed her watching him, and turned and gave her a smile that sent shivers down to Lucia's toes. As she smiled back, Harrison felt warmth spread through his veins. Tonight Lucia radiated loveliness, and he had delighted in watching her shine.

King Easton was right. After seeing all sides of Lucia, he could see what was irrefutable. Tonight was her night, and she glowed.

She'd conversed easily with the Arab sheikh's wife, and she'd easily held her own against the movie star with the three Oscars.

Yes, Lucia would make an ideal queen for Korosol. He pushed those thoughts out of his mind. These next few days he needed to concentrate simply on her, and their remaining time together before Easton's announcement that would set the future in stone.

But tonight, he also knew one other fact. Never had he felt prouder, or more in love.

It would be the hardest duty of his life to let her go.

"Did a ghost cross your path?"

"What?" Harrison turned as Lucia walked up. Her elegant red dress swished around her feet.

"A ghost. You looked as if you suddenly had a horrible thought." She put her fingers lightly on his arm and looked at him.

He had, but he wouldn't ruin her night by telling her about it.

"No, I didn't," he said. He smiled. "I'm enjoying myself."

"Good. We'll be here a lot this weekend. I'm doing a lecture tomorrow at noon. A lunch-hour show, so to speak."

"Sounds interesting," Harrison said.

"Not really," Lucia said. Then using Pam's words she said, "I'd rather be hiding out in our room. I'm sure we could find other ways to occupy our time."

Her spoken desire assaulted his brain, causing blood to pool lower. "Shh," he said, shifting to hide his reaction. "Time for that later."

"Is it later yet?" She turned her face up to his, and Harrison found himself wishing he could kiss the tip of her nose. If they'd been any other couple, he would have. Here it was too public, too risky.

"Soon," he said, for once wishing time would move just a little bit faster. He touched his hands to hers, feeling the electricity pass between them.

"I'll hold you to that," Lucia said. Her green

eyes sent him a kiss as she moved away to speak with a woman Pam was bringing over.

Finally, around nine, Lucia deemed it time to leave. "Pam will close up," she said. "If we don't leave now, the party will last forever."

"We don't want that," he agreed, her subtle meaning clear.

"I want our own party to last forever," Lucia said. "So shall we say our goodbyes?"

Harrison couldn't agree with her more.

Forty minutes later, he found his anticipation growing as they entered the inn lobby. Starting with tonight, he wanted these next few nights to be absolutely perfect for Lucia.

Thus he had arranged a special surprise for her.

He inserted the key into the lock and opened the door to their suite for her. As she stepped in, he heard her gasp in astonishment.

"It's lovely. Oh, Harrison."

Smiling, he stepped inside the room and closed the door behind him.

LUCIA DIDN'T NEED to reach for the light switch to see the romantic surprise Harrison had created for her.

He'd created heaven.

Candles flickering everywhere revealed a room filled with red roses. Rose petals made a trail from the door to the turned-down bed where a single red rose rested on the white pillowcase. Dozens of roses in vases decorated the room, filling it with the fresh scent of an English garden.

A fire burned brightly in the fireplace grate, and Lucia turned to Harrison. "You always remind me of roses," he said.

Lucia saw his hazel eyes lightly mist over. "My favorite flower," she said.

"Of course," he replied. He traced her nose with his finger. "Everything about you is imprinted on my heart."

"No one has ever done anything like this for me before," she said. Slight tears of happiness watered her eyes and she blinked them back. "Kiss me."

"An order I'd follow any day," he replied. He meant every single word.

Lucia reveled in the feel of his lips touching down on hers. Each perfect touch made her quiver; every touch of his tongue made her experience the sweetest nectar of the gods.

His tuxedo needed to go, and Lucia planted kisses on Harrison's neck as she began to unfasten his bow tie.

"Slow," he told her.

She nodded, understanding his need to savor the moment, to draw it out and make it last forever. In the magical world they'd created they had all the time they would ever need.

No quick coupling was necessary. Tonight their

lovemaking would be a union of two souls that needed to come together to complete their destiny.

So they stroked, kissed, teased, until finally, Harrison flipped the covers aside and made sweet delicate love to Lucia on the remnants of the rose petals that were scattered on the bed.

"Oh yes," she found herself saying aloud as he glided himself inside her awaiting body. Stars detonated, resonated, and she slivered into delicate pieces of the most valuable gold.

Together they had found their own piece of nirvana. As she held him joined inside her, Lucia couldn't imagine ever losing their perfect union. The memory of it would be engraved on her soul forever.

A single tear slid slowly down her cheek.

"You're crying," Harrison said. He fingered the tear, and brought the wetness to his lips.

"I'm just happy," she replied, for indeed she was. "I can't imagine anything ever being more perfect."

"Me neither," Harrison replied. He dropped butterfly kisses on her nose, and deep inside her body she felt him stir.

"Thank you," she told him, for those words she could say to him. Her love was a secret she could never reveal, words she could never say aloud.

He slowly stroked her cheek with the back of his fingers. "I should be thanking you, Lucia."

"Why?"

He leaned down and kissed her forehead before replying, "You taught me how to feel again, how to let myself be free."

Lucia blinked back new tears. When had loving him become so hard? "You were always free, Harrison. You just hid it under that tough exterior and your devotion to duty. You've always had this capacity to feel and love deep within you."

"I didn't know it until I met you," he said. "You've completed me."

Lucia stroked his back, memorizing the feel of his skin. She traced ridges, tiny scars, and just the texture of his taut muscles.

"We're good together," she said, for in the flickering candlelight she could be honest about that one thing. "I'll forever treasure these moments we've spent together. They've been some of the best of my life."

Harrison said nothing, but instead he brought his mouth down on hers in a fervor that startled Lucia. Still joined together, she felt him move deep within her.

As he began stoking the flame higher, she kissed him right back. The intensity in their sudden need to make love again said it all, said the words that neither believed they could ever voice to each other.

Lucia held him, loved him, and cried out with the joy and passion of the perfect lovemaking. This was her man, and she fit him perfectly. Every moment she could spend with him was one to be cherished.

Finally, desire satiated, they held each other. After his breathing became regular, Lucia stroked Harrison's face.

His arm heavy over hers, she memorized the feel of the weight of it, absorbed the delicious prickliness of skin resting on skin.

She pressed a kiss to his shoulder, and then, with her eyelids closing, she curled her body farther against his.

Sleep was quick in claiming her, but not before Harrison's arms drew her as close as humanly possible. He fitted her to him, spooning her into his side.

As sleep found him, peace and contentment descended in the room. Firelight flickered, casting a romantic glow over the lovers.

In this position Lucia felt as if nothing could ever go wrong. Even becoming queen of Korosol would somehow be okay.

Contented, she drifted away into a dreamless, heavenly sleep.

Chapter Eleven

For once, King Easton wished he could be a night person. Instead, he was one of those type-A people that rose early and hit the day at full speed.

Today he wished he hadn't.

He tossed the newspaper aside and frowned. Betrayal. That's what it was, absolute betrayal by a member of the royal family.

He glanced up, seeing Sir Devon, his loyal captain of the Royal Guard, standing in front of him. The boy had mettle, which was a good thing.

Easton had never needed to rely on Devon before, and he knew the young man was going to need all his strength to complete this particular job.

Finally everything made perfect sense.

"Thank you for bringing the circumstances surrounding the Katwell matter to my attention so promptly," Easton said, carefully choosing his words. "I need Harrison back here so I can deal with this. Please go to Aspen and retrieve him and

Lucia immediately. It's not wise to phone. I will fill him in on the circumstances when he gets here.''

"Yes, Your Grace." Devon nodded, and Easton wondered if he'd learned from his father how to school his features into a mask.

Dismissing Devon before he could make the required bow, Easton swiveled the chair and stared out the window of his office at the embassy. Today drizzle hid the Manhattan skyline in a dismal gray haze that cloaked everything and made the beautiful city seem ugly.

Never before had he felt more homesick. He wanted his palace, his beautiful countryside.

And he wanted that wonderful land that he'd loved since his birth to be left in good hands. Thus he didn't want to think about what had happened, or what he knew he had to do. Yes, he knew he should have stayed in bed this morning.

Betrayal to Korosol was just the tip of the iceberg he'd have to deal with today. The personal betrayal, and finding out the truth, hurt the most. Easton put his head in his hands as, behind Devon, the door finally latched with an ominous click.

FOR HARRISON, Saturday morning dawned all too soon. He and Lucia had been sharing a bed for the past three nights. Sleeping in heaven couldn't have been sweeter, unless Lucia would be there to curl up around him.

"Come on, sleepyhead," he whispered into her ear. They'd spent Friday night locked in their suite simply making love, and he was surprised she could even blink her eyes. But she had an appointment at the gallery, and she needed to wake up and get ready to leave.

He leaned up on one arm and used a forefinger to stroke her cheek.

"Don't wanna," Lucia mumbled. Under his teasing touch her tiredness faded and she reached up. She pulled him down to kiss her. "Let's stay in," she suggested, her voice husky with the remnants of sleep.

"You've got an appointment," he told her in between her sensual kisses.

"Cancel it," Lucia murmured, the touch of her body against his already causing him to respond.

Harrison groaned. His woman was absolutely insatiable, not that he minded. But right now they couldn't indulge their need.

"Not now, sweetheart," he told her. As much as he didn't want to, he pulled back away from her roving hands. "You need to wake up and get ready. You need to be there, darling. No playing hooky," he teased. "It's your show, remember?"

"Oh, all right," Lucia said. She rolled over, giving Harrison a view of her perfectly rounded bottom. He groaned, for as always, he wanted her with a passion that showed no sign of ever lessening.

"Stop tempting me and get up," he ordered lovingly. "We've already slept in too late. It's ten."

Lucia sat up with a start, her green eyes wide. "What? I've got to be there at eleven."

Harrison wanted to laugh at how cute she looked. Her blond hair was tousled and her lips were still swollen from the heat of last night's kisses.

"Exactly. Get moving, darling."

SOMEHOW THEY MANAGED to arrive promptly at the gallery at eleven. Lucia had insisted they shower together, and of course it had taken longer than just soaping up and rinsing off. Once inside the shower, it was inevitable that they had to make love under the cascading water droplets.

"I'm going to check out the shop next door," Harrison told her. "I'll meet you back here in an hour and we'll go to lunch."

Lucia reached up and gave him a kiss. She'd become bolder, not caring who saw how she felt about him. "Sounds delightful."

"You are so lucky," Pam said as Lucia entered the art gallery. "I wish I could find a man like that."

I wish I could keep a man like that, Lucia thought as she watched Harrison move down the sidewalk toward another shop. Soon he disappeared from view. But Sunday would be here tomorrow, with the press conference announcing her as the next queen of Korosol to be held the following day. The hourglass sand was almost out of magic.

She smiled at Pam, keeping her sad thoughts inside. "You'll find someone," she told her.

"I hope so," Pam replied. "As long as he doesn't turn out to be a jerk like my ex was, then it'll be an improvement."

Lucia forgot about the conversation until shortly after she and Harrison had eaten lunch at a small microbrewery. The food had been delicious.

Since Lucia only had one appointment after lunch, Harrison remained in the art gallery while Lucia finished the piece for a customer who had scheduled the appointment over four months ago.

"Beautiful," the woman remarked. She turned her wrist and the precious gems reflected the light. "I am so impressed. This is exactly what I wanted. You do such wonderful work."

"Thank you," Lucia said. She stretched her neck and removed the small eyepiece she'd been wearing in her right eye.

This was it. Her last client of the weekend. She and Harrison were finally free to leave and Lucia couldn't wait. She had plans for the afternoon and they didn't include skiing.

"Lucia." Pam came into the anteroom where Lucia was working. "There's a man outside who looks just like Harrison. If you know him, please introduce me."

Lucia glanced at Harrison. There was only one person who looked like Harrison, and he was in New York. Harrison strode over to Lucia's side. "Pam, what are you talking about?"

"There's a man asking for you out in the foyer. He looks like—"

Pam didn't have a chance to finish as the younger version of Harrison walked into the room. "There you both are."

"This is a private area," Pam said, for no matter what a person looked like, it was a business. "I told you to wait out in the—"

"It's okay." Harrison's authoritative voice filled the room. Lucia turned and stared at him.

Devon's sudden appearance in the art gallery had her worried. The only reason he would have come to Aspen was that something had to have happened. Her fears escalated when she looked out into the main gallery and saw other members of the Royal Guard milling about.

"Pam, will you please leave us?" Lucia saw her friend's eyes widen at Harrison's request.

"It's fine," she reassured her. Pam stepped out of the room.

"Easton wants to see you back in New York immediately," Devon said bluntly the moment Pam was out of earshot.

"What?" Harrison's shock was obvious.

"We need to leave now. There's a helicopter

waiting to take us to the airport where the royal jet is on standby.'' Devon's face revealed nothing, gave them no indication of what was wrong.

Lucia's instinct told her whatever it was, it wasn't good. ''Are you going to tell us what this is about?'' Lucia said.

''I'm not privileged to have that information,'' Devon said, and Lucia had the impression that even if he did know what it was, he wasn't going to say.

''I have no idea what is going on,'' Harrison told Lucia. They sat in the back of a limousine taking them to a heliport.

''I'm worried,'' she replied. ''Something's terribly wrong.''

''It'll be okay,'' Harrison promised her. ''Whatever it is, I'll take care of it. Trust me.''

''I will,'' she said, for she did. She wished she could touch him. Since she couldn't do that, she wished she could at least hold his hand, but with Devon sitting in the front she knew that she couldn't.

Their magical world's security had been breached, and the hourglass had broken.

Lucia frowned. Whatever the reason was had to be serious. They hadn't even been allowed to return to the inn for their belongings.

Devon had sent some Royal Guard members after their belongings. That thought made Lucia wince. She hadn't had time to straighten the room after her and Harrison's earlier lovemaking, and the room probably still had lingerie strewn all over. The maid didn't clean until three.

Lucia tried not to worry as the helicopter flew them into Denver. She failed.

"CAN'T YOU TELL ME what is going on?" Harrison looked at his son. They were in the front compartment of the private jet, and Harrison had approached Devon.

"I wish I could, but I'm under orders not to," Devon replied. He glanced away, and Harrison knew immediately that whatever it was had something to do with him.

"Devon," he said. Devon looked up. "I know I haven't been a good father to you."

Devon said nothing, and Harrison paused. "You've made me very proud, son, but this has nothing to do with you. I know how much you love your job, and how good you are at it. But I've learned something this weekend. Duty isn't everything. Family has to come first."

"Amazing you learn that when you need something from me," Devon said.

Harrison winced. He deserved that. "Someone had to teach it to me. Isn't learning it late better than not learning it at all?"

"I saw your hotel room," Devon said.

Harrison nodded. "So you know."

"Easton does too, although not to that extent."

"I care for her a great deal. I know you had your heart set on being prince consort, and I'm sorry. I didn't try to take your place."

"I don't want Princess Lucia." Devon looked at his father. "What gave you that idea? I know King Easton wants it, but neither she nor I do. That's not the real issue here."

"Then tell me what is," Harrison said.

Devon studied his father. "Do you love her or were you just carried away doing your duty?"

"I love her," Harrison said simply. He did, too, and it pained him to no end. He and Lucia could love each other all they wanted, but they could never be together.

If he knew his king, and he did, their next meeting would be terrible. Death would be easier.

"Krissy Katwell wrote a tabloid article. She had a picture of the two of you kissing. It's on the front page and there's no doubt that it's you and Lucia. King Easton saw it first thing this morning."

"Thank you for telling me," Harrison said.

Devon shook his head, indicating the conversation was over. Harrison returned to his seat. At the other end of the main passenger compartment Lucia thumbed through a magazine. He wanted to go to her, but he knew he couldn't. Not with the royal guard staring at him.

He'd failed his duty. He'd failed his code of honor, all for the woman he loved.

It was too late to get any of that back. All he could do was protect her. He would do it, and he would do whatever was necessary.

That would be whatever the king wanted.

A FEW HOURS LATER, Devon returned from the cockpit of the Korosolan private jet.

"King Easton phoned the plane, and because of the time change, he's asked us to meet him at Charlotte's apartment," Devon said.

From her seat a distance away from him, Lucia saw Harrison nod. "How much longer until we arrive?" he asked.

"We're beginning our initial descent now," Devon replied.

The way he didn't quite look at his father sent a shiver through Lucia. Could Devon know?

They were at Charlotte's apartment less than an hour later.

"Lucia, how could you?" her mother said as they entered. "I had more faith in you. You've disappointed me again."

Lucia glanced at her mother. Charlotte's lips had puckered into a disapproving line. Lucia frowned. Just what was going on? Fear filled her. Did they know about her and Harrison?

If they did, would it really matter?

She didn't have time to think about it as Devon showed them into Charlotte's private study.

"Easton asks that you remain outside," Devon said to Charlotte, and then shut the door. Her mother remained in the hall.

I feel as if I'm about to face an inquisition, Lucia thought. She wished she could share her thoughts with Harrison, but she could tell he'd already withdrawn into his facade of duty.

He said he'd take care of it, and that scared her even more. She knew he would go to whatever lengths necessary to protect her, even at a cost to himself. She didn't want him to suffer in any way.

Devon stood at attention by the inside of the door as Lucia and Harrison approached the large mahogany desk Easton had commandeered.

Easton had his back to them. Suddenly he swung around in the chair to face them.

Lucia had never seen her grandfather appear so old. His skin appeared more wrinkled, his green eyes tired and worn. Had he aged that much in the little less than a week she had been gone?

"I've called you both back here because of a matter you may not be aware of," Easton said. "It has to do with betrayal of trust, trust I placed in you."

His gaze indicated Harrison, and Lucia turned to face the man she loved. She saw him pale.

"Therefore," Easton continued, "I am hereby

relieving you of all your duties and your titles unless you marry my granddaughter immediately.''

"What!" The words that burst forth angrily came from her own mouth. Forgetting her grandfather was a king, Lucia took a step forward. "Excuse me for sounding rude, but just what are you talking about?"

"This," Easton replied. He unfolded the newspaper in front of him. There, on page seven of the *Manhattan Chronicle* was a huge picture of Lucia and Harrison. The headline said it all: Simply Scandalous Princess Finds Snow Body.

The body of Krissy Katwell's story told about Lucia's love affair with an older man who happened to work for her grandfather.

"Oh my God," Lucia said. She drew in a breath and sunk into a nearby chair.

Who had taken that picture? It was of them kissing after their impromptu snowball fight. The ski patrolwoman's words came back into Lucia's memory. The woman had said she thought she'd seen someone else near the end of the slope. Lucia realized the woman actually had seen someone.

"I trusted you to behave yourself like a man of your rank and stature should," Easton said. "You have failed me, Harrison."

Harrison's face remained a mask as he took Easton's censure. Seeing Harrison having to endure such discipline from his king filled Lucia with pain.

Worse, the emotions she'd worked so hard to free had retreated beneath his armor of duty.

"It's not his fault," Lucia inserted quickly. She tried to deflect her grandfather's anger. "It's mine. I initiated everything."

Easton didn't seem to hear her, or if he did he didn't seem to care. "It doesn't matter," he said. "Lucia was raised in America, so that can excuse her not knowing any better. However, Harrison, you are Korosolan. You were supposed to see if she had any skeletons, not help her create them."

"Yes, Your Grace. I was wrong." Harrison bowed his head in shame.

Easton tapped a pen on the desk; the noise was the only sound filling the room for several long seconds.

"You will marry my granddaughter immediately," Easton finally decreed. "I will not have this embarrassment tarnish or sully her reputation. We will simply announce you two secretly became engaged this weekend. It will fit in well with my announcement of Lucia as my heir."

"Yes, Your Grace." Harrison stood tall.

"Good. So you will marry her." Easton nodded his approval.

"Yes, Your Grace."

Although Harrison's voice sounded strong, Lucia still winced. Without question he'd accepted

Easton's words as law, no matter what she might happen to think about the matter.

"Excellent," Easton said with another approving nod. "I gave this a lot of thought on your journey back here and I feel that this will be the best solution for everyone, especially for you, Harrison. I did not want to dismiss you in disgrace. You've been too loyal to Korosol for far too many years to let your entire military career end like this."

"Yes, sir."

Fury filled Lucia at Harrison's acceptance of their fate. He was trying to protect her, she knew that. But she'd been taking care of herself for years. She didn't need his help. She was not Mary.

She would not let her grandfather do this.

Chapter Twelve

"No." The word spit forth from her mouth.

Both men instantly turned and looked at her, their surprise evident.

"What do you mean, no?" Easton frowned. No one dared to question his decisions, but Lucia knew she wasn't just anyone.

She was a strong woman of integrity. Despite what anyone in her family might think, or how disappointed they might be, she chose her own destiny.

She always had, and she wasn't about to change her mind or her patterns now, even if it meant not being queen of Korosol.

So what if her actions disappointed her mother? Her mother, like all the other times, would get over it. This was Lucia's life, and she'd carved it out for herself. In the end, it was she that had to be happy with her actions. She would not let Harrison pay for them.

"I said no, and my no means no. I will not marry Harrison." The name of the man she loved quivered on her tongue slightly, but she got it out without a stutter.

In reality she'd love to marry Harrison. She'd love nothing more than to be his wife and bear his children.

She would not marry him like this. He would not be forced to marry her because of duty. While she wanted to be his second wife, she wanted to be nothing like his first.

If he married her, she wanted it to be because Harrison loved her, not because he felt responsible for tarnishing her reputation.

Marriage should be about love and passion, not about duty and being honorable.

"Of course you will marry him," Easton said, interpreting her long silence as a need for his reassurance. "Your reputation will be tarnished if you don't marry him, and after your sisters, I won't have that for the future queen."

Now she was like her sisters. How often had she heard that growing up?

Lucia jutted her chin forward. One of her traits inherited from her father was stubbornness, and for a moment she had sudden insight into why Drake traveled the world to get out of Korosol. He'd loved his father, but he'd needed to be his own man.

"I will not marry Harrison. Especially not under

these circumstances," Lucia said. She planted her hands on her hips. "This is the twenty-first century, not the fifteenth, Grandfather. I will not be married off because of some trashy newspaper article Krissy Katwell wrote. People will forget all about it tomorrow."

"No, they won't," Easton said. His look was pained, as if he found her rebellion unsettling. "You are going to be a queen. The press will feast on this. Is it too much to ask that your affair be proper?"

Lucia winced slightly as her grandfather continued. "Besides, if you are as interested in Harrison as the newspaper clipping maintains, would being married to him be such a bad thing? You've obviously showed him more attention than you have ever shown Devon."

"I've never wanted Devon," Lucia said.

"Exactly," Easton replied.

He just didn't understand. Couldn't he see that Harrison was only marrying her out of duty? That wasn't a foundation of a relationship. Sure, she loved him, but he didn't love her. He'd always resent her for taking away his choice, and his freedom to have decided for himself.

Lucia's frustration reached a pinnacle. She couldn't marry Harrison. And he couldn't marry her. Not out of duty.

She would not let it happen.

She would only marry for love.

"No." Her voice strengthened as her resolve solidified. "Grandfather, I love you, but you cannot force me to marry Harrison."

"You will, if you are to be queen."

"Then I won't be queen," Lucia said.

Easton paled slightly and Lucia hated wounding him. She despised having to take this harsh stance.

"That's not an option. Harrison will lose his job if you do not."

Lucia gripped the edge of her chair. At Easton's proclamation she tried to make eye contact with Harrison. His face revealed nothing. Her heart shattered.

"I do not believe you will fire him, Grandfather."

His bluff called, Easton said, "Can't you see that I just want you and Harrison to be proper?"

Lucia straightened her shoulders. This was going to be one of the hardest things she'd ever do in her life. "I love you, Grandfather, and I don't want to disappoint you. But I will not be married off to someone just because you desire it to be proper."

Without waiting for a reply or a dismissal, Lucia rose and went to the door. Devon hesitated a moment, and Lucia thought she saw admiration in his eyes. Then he stepped aside and let her pass.

Her mother hovered in the hallway, her mouth already open to speak.

Lucia made the first strike. "I'm not discussing it with you," she told her mother simply. She jabbed the elevator button. Time to go home and lick her wounds.

"I heard everything," Charlotte said, practically running to keep up with Lucia's fast stride. "How could you, Lucia? You must marry Harrison."

Charlotte's look pleaded with Lucia to change her mind and be sensible. Lucia ignored it.

"Don't you understand that your whole future is riding on this? Lucia, you've angered your grandfather. Whatever words you two might have exchanged, I'm sure you can fix it. Just do as he wishes."

Lucia stopped so fast that Charlotte almost ran into her back. She turned to her mother. "No."

"Lucia!" Charlotte's face visibly whitened and she put her hand on the pearls at her throat. Her knuckles tensed as she twisted them.

Lucia pushed aside the guilt at disappointing her mother. She did love her, but her mother just didn't understand. This was a matter of the heart. There was no compromise, and whatever she did, she could not back down.

"No, Mother. I'm sorry, but that isn't possible. This is my life," Lucia said firmly. "Please understand that while I don't want to hurt you, I must make my own decisions, especially about this."

And with that, Lucia walked into the open elevator and punched the button for the lobby. She cried all the way home.

IN THE STUDY, Easton stared at the open door. No one had ever walked out on him, except Drake. Now Drake's daughter had. Despite himself, he had to admire her spirit.

"Close the door and leave us a moment," he ordered Devon.

Devon immediately obeyed, and Easton found himself finally alone with Harrison.

"Easton, I am sorry," Harrison said the first moment he could.

Easton waved his hand as if brushing the matter aside. "I just want it proper, Harrison."

"I understand," Harrison replied.

Easton knew Harrison well enough to know that he did understand. He studied the man who had stood by his side for two decades of his life.

"Do you love her?" Easton finally asked. He suspected the answer, but he wanted confirmation. He wanted to hear the truth for himself.

"Yes." Harrison bent his head.

Easton savored the truth for a moment, although knowing it didn't ease the feeling of betrayal by his closest friend. He swallowed, taking time to choose his words carefully. "Why didn't you say anything? Have we not been together long enough for you to trust me?"

Harrison folded his hands and placed them in his lap as he sat down in the chair Lucia had vacated. "You kept setting her up with Devon."

Easton smiled slightly as he realized what Harrison must have been going through. The man was loyal, and would do anything for his king despite the pain. He'd even stopped an assassin's bullet, and because of it had spent a year recovering. "It must have bothered you to have seen Lucia being set up as a partner to your son."

"Horribly," Harrison admitted.

"So if you feel this way toward her, can't you get her to marry you?"

Harrison shook his head, and Easton felt disappointed. "I'd marry her in a heartbeat, but she'll never trust that I'm telling her the truth. She'll think I'm marrying her out of duty. She's too stubborn to believe me now."

Easton sighed. He suddenly felt extremely tired and he tried to remember if he'd taken his medicine. The doctors who had diagnosed his disease had told him to avoid stress. He wished he could, but with his feisty granddaughters it was not that simple.

"I just don't want any more scandal. She's going to be queen," Easton said. "Although, whether she'll be at the press conference tomorrow isn't a certainty. Call Ellie and have her postpone it. I want more time to resolve this matter before I invite a press feeding frenzy."

"I'll do that." Harrison rose to his feet.

"You need to convince her to marry you," Easton said again. "That would solve everything."

For the second time that day someone defied Easton. "I can't," Harrison replied, a look of sadness covering his face. "I must let her be free."

As much as he hated it, Easton understood. For one time in his life, Harrison had just chosen love over loyalty to Korosol.

Easton knew his friend was in pain, and Easton prided himself on being a reasonable and benevolent monarch. "You can keep your job as my adviser, but from this moment on you are to have nothing further to do with Princess Lucia."

"One meeting—"

"No," Easton said.

"Agreed." Harrison winced as the word left his mouth.

Easton sighed and reached slowly for the water goblet in front of him. His medicine made him thirsty, and he wished his hand didn't shake so much. "You're free to go, Harrison."

He saw Harrison nod and bow. Then he looked again at his king. The unspoken question was in his eyes, and Easton knew exactly what Harrison wanted.

Without hesitation Easton picked up the newspaper. He knew Harrison kept a small box of me-

mentos. Now he'd have the photograph of him and Lucia. "Take it. Just trash the article."

"Thank you. I will."

As Harrison opened the door to leave, Easton twirled the chair around without another word.

WHO SAID grown men don't cry? While he wouldn't shed tears, he'd love to be able to do so.

Harrison strode through Charlotte's apartment, his mind in a haze.

He, Sir Harrison Montcalm, had just lost everything he loved. Lucia and his job didn't mix, wouldn't ever mix, and he could never have her. He was lucky he even had a job at all.

"There you are." Charlotte pounced on Harrison before he reached the foyer. He'd hoped for a quick escape. "I want to know what are you going to do about my daughter."

Harrison drew himself up. Charlotte had the right to be angry. "I'm following Easton's orders, ma'am."

"Good." Charlotte nodded. "I overheard. Since you won't marry her, that would be for the best."

Better for everyone, including Lucia.

But not better for him.

Lucia had taught him to feel. She had taught him to love. She had freed his emotions.

Because of Lucia he had opened his Pandora's

box. That meant one thing. Every emotion he'd long ago locked away deep inside had escaped.

Even hope was gone.

Losing Lucia, letting her go, meant one thing.

He'd hurt for a long time.

Chapter Thirteen

"Life isn't all roses at the Korosolan embassy."

"Really?" Markus turned as his right-hand man entered the exclusive men's club in Midtown.

More than one week after the canceled press conference, Winston Rademacher was still the bearer of good news. Markus took a puff on his cigar.

"Everyone at the embassy is in limbo. Princess Lucia has refused to answer any phone calls or let anyone up to her loft," Winston said. He sat down in an armchair and kicked his feet up on an ottoman. "It seems she's become a recluse. I heard the doorman even had to turn away her mother."

Markus reached for his scotch. He took a long swallow. "So loving Harrison Montcalm sent the good princess into hiding."

"Perhaps he really is of some use after all to the throne," Winston said with a sneer. "We didn't have to do anything but send out a photographer after her."

"Yes, Harrison actually did something useful in sleeping with her. I wouldn't have thought the old man had it in him."

Markus let the liquid burn down his throat. He waved at the private club's waitress. "Another," he said when she approached.

And why not?

Winston had just brought such good news. Easton had run out of granddaughters, and he'd have to end this foolish notion of his of finding a different heir besides Markus.

Now the throne would be returning where it rightfully belonged—to him.

"Keep on top of the situation," Markus said. He took another puff of his cigar. "I wouldn't want the old man to pull any surprises out of his hat."

"I'm always on top of everything," Winston said with the confidence of a man who was.

Markus sipped his third scotch of the hour. "Keep it that way. We'll go ahead as if Lucia is still in the picture."

Winston nodded. "Of course. Chance may be on our side, but we shouldn't risk it. We could have too much to lose if we don't."

"YOU MAY GO right in." Ellie rose from her seat.

"Are you certain?" Devon asked. "I'm early."

Ellie watched as Sir Devon entered King Easton's outer office. She'd always liked Devon.

He was a good man. Too bad about the mess with his father. She'd always liked Sir Harrison.

"King Easton has been expecting you. He'll be glad that you're early."

"Hopefully I'm bringing him good news." Devon did look a bit optimistic, Ellie decided. She certainly wanted some good news.

Ever since Lucia and Harrison's early return from Aspen and the subsequent scandal, life around the embassy had been stilted at best. The only one who ever appeared chipper was Prince Markus.

Devon paused at Ellie's desk. She pushed her glasses back up her nose. "So what is your news? I can tell you that the only news King Easton wants is that Princess Lucia will schedule a press conference. It's been a week and a half and she's still not speaking to anyone, including the king."

"That news I don't have." Devon frowned for a moment as if he was contemplating something. "Have you seen my father lately?"

"Yesterday," Ellie said with a slight shrug. "He's kept a low profile since the tabloid article. If you need him I bet he's in his office. He's pretty much holed up there unless Easton requests him to come up here."

"How's Harrison doing?"

It had always seemed odd to Ellie that Devon always referred to his father by his given name. She would have thought they would have grown closer over the years, but that hadn't happened. Maybe this incident over Lucia would, in the end, draw them together.

She spoke carefully. "I think your father's still licking his wounds, so to speak."

"He really cares for her." Devon made the statement as if it was an irrefutable fact. Ellie was surprised. Devon had confirmed her suspicions.

Ellie pushed a strand of her brown hair off her face. Normally she didn't gossip, but Devon needed to bridge whatever gap he had with his father. "I think so. He certainly looks like a man who has lost everything. I think he loves her. I mean, he risked so much."

Devon nodded and Ellie wished she knew what he was thinking. He kept his thoughts private. "I'd better get in there," Devon said, indicating Easton's office. "Thanks for the update."

"Sure," Ellie said. She sat back down at her desk and watched him enter.

When King Easton had first proposed this trip, he'd promised that it would be a lot of fun. "You'll be able to shop, take in museums, see a play on Broadway," he'd told Ellie.

She'd been excited at the prospect of visiting what tourists called the Big Apple, although she'd learned the natives certainly didn't call it that.

But the working vacation she'd been hoping for had turned out to be all work and no vacation. Well, if she didn't count one shopping trip to a designer salon for CeCe's wedding gown.

She'd been tied to this very office ever since they'd arrived in February. At least it had a large window, or Ellie would never see the outside at all. Her living quarters were in the embassy building as well, and the grand trip to New York that Easton had promised her was actually simply just another day, now two months, at the office.

She sighed. Oh well, as soon as this mess with Princess Lucia straightened itself out, Ellie would at least get to go home.

After all, she wasn't getting any younger.

LUCIA PRESSED the buzzer on her phone. "Yes?"

"Miss Carradigne?"

"Yes." Lucia tried to calm her tone. She didn't want to sound too irritated at the unwelcome interruption. It had been several days since the last person had attempted to contact her.

Poor Frank had been a sport about her short temper. He'd turned away everyone who had tried to see her, including her mother.

"You have a package here," Frank told her. His voice came clearly across the in-house line. "It's legitimate. The deliveryman was from Saks Fifth Avenue."

"Saks?" She hadn't ordered anything, so who

would be sending her anything from Saks? "I'll send the elevator down."

As part of the loft's security features, Lucia could, and had, locked the elevator up at her floor. Within moments the package had arrived, and she relocked the elevator.

"Now, what's this?" Lucia took out a pair of scissors and began to open what turned out to be a dress box.

Inside was a fire-red ball gown. Lucia held the dress up. Not quite what she would have picked out for herself, but it was pretty. She tossed the garment over the back of the sofa.

She lifted the envelope that was in the package. The dress was a gift from Markus. Her cousin had written:

My dearest Lucia,
I was shopping today, and immediately when I saw this I thought of you. Plus, with all that is going on in your life I thought you could use some cheering up. Please wear it to the Inferno Ball and save me some dances. In this dress you'll be the belle of the ball. I look forward to seeing you,
Markus.

Lucia folded the card and put it back in the envelope. Markus had sent her a dress.

Was she so pathetic that now everyone was trying to make her feel better?

She moved over to her workbench. Everyone probably thought she needed to have her head examined. She'd hidden out for over a week, only eating after her stomach demanded food. She'd showered, but she'd lived in her sweat clothes instead of ever dressing even in what her mother called her "bohemian attire."

Mostly, though, she'd worked. She'd created piece after piece of jewelry. They were her most vivid, boldest pieces yet, as if reflecting the turmoil and anger of the woman creating them.

She wanted Harrison. She didn't want to be queen. But fate had gotten it wrong and twisted it up. She would be queen. She wouldn't have Harrison.

No one ever said life was fair.

She wondered if Harrison still had his beloved job. She closed her eyes. Being queen would ensure that he'd always be able to do what he loved.

And he loved Korosol. More than her.

And she loved him more than Korosol. At least one of them would be happy.

At least she could give him that.

Lucia reached forward and fingered the small tie tack she'd made. A tear fell from her eye and she angrily brushed it away.

Long ago in some long-forgotten history class,

she'd learned that, as a child, Catherine the Great of Russia had watched her favorite pet eat poisoned food. As part of her training, Catherine hadn't been allowed to show any emotion while the dog had died right in front of her.

To the outside world, what Lucia was being asked to do wasn't anything like what young Catherine had suffered.

To her heart, it felt the same.

Harrison was dead to her. Worse, she'd be able to see him and know that she couldn't have him, couldn't hold him, couldn't love him.

There was no greater torture than that.

She'd never run from anything before, and she knew she was running now. Destiny would eventually catch her, it always did. That much she knew. She might as well face her date with destiny head-on.

She picked up her phone and dialed the number she'd written on a pad by the phone.

"Eleanor Standish," she said to the receptionist at the Korosolan embassy.

ELLIE PUT the phone down and practically jumped for joy. Finally a light at the end of the tunnel had appeared…and it wasn't a train.

It had been two days since Devon had visited and, without knocking, a very excited Eleanor burst into King Easton's office. "Lucia's agreed to do the press conference,'' Ellie announced without preamble. "I've already contacted Sir Devon and requested he come straight here. She wants it for this afternoon at four.''

Easton's jaw hung open and he quickly closed it. He'd never thought Ellie had it in her to be so spontaneous. No time to contemplate that. Lucia had broken her silence and finally called.

"She's agreed?'' Easton questioned, just to be sure his old ears hadn't heard it wrong.

"Yes.'' Ellie smiled. She loved to be the bearer of good news.

"She's going to be queen?'' Easton wanted to be perfectly certain. Charlotte's daughters hadn't been too reliable.

"Yes,'' Ellie replied. Her excitement was infectious. "Her exact words were 'I might as well get it over with. Set it up for four.'''

"That would be a yes,'' Easton said. Relief filled him. If he'd learned anything about his granddaughter Lucia, she would do what she said. Hadn't she proved that by hiding out for over a week?

Yes, if she was coming, and holding a press conference, he had an heir.

A knock on the door told him that Devon had arrived. "Your Grace.'' Devon entered and bowed quickly. "I'll get right on the security arrangements.''

"Good," Easton said. He felt as if a burden had been lifted from him.

Easton glanced out the window, which he often did when something was bothering him. By all intents he should be radiantly happy.

He wasn't. Something was still bothering him.

The something else that was bothering him walked through the door right at that moment.

"Your Grace." Harrison Montcalm executed a perfect bow. "You told me to bring the papers the moment they were finished."

"Yes, yes." Easton's impatience built. Right now he didn't care about the papers outlining a new trade alliance. He gestured to a table. "Put them over there."

Harrison looked surprised but followed the king's direction. Easton spoke to Ellie before he dismissed her. "Ellie, have Charlotte's PR agency alert the media. Close the door behind you on your way out."

"Yes, Your Grace," Ellie said. Within seconds the three men were alone.

"Lucia has agreed to hold the conference today at four," Easton told Harrison. As his friend of many years nodded, Easton watched Harrison's face. It remained neutral. Easton sighed. Harrison had given so many loyal years to the throne. He deserved to be happy.

"I'm stepping up security," Devon told them.

"I've received absolute proof of what we already believed to be true. Rademacher is definitely Krissy Katwell's source. He's behind every one of the leaks, including hiring the photographer who snapped the picture of Princess Lucia and Harrison."

Easton heard Harrison's sharp intake of breath. "Have you made any ties to Markus?" Easton asked.

Devon turned and answered the king's question. "No. So far we don't have any conclusive proof that Rademacher isn't just working by himself. We've got some of our best men working on it."

"Keep me informed," Easton said. "And be sure that security is tight. I don't want anything to go wrong today. If Rademacher is this involved, he may be getting desperate, especially if we are about to announce Lucia as the new queen."

"Nothing will happen on my watch," Devon promised. He rose. "If Your Grace doesn't need me I'd like to personally supervise the preparations."

"Excellent," Easton said. He turned to Harrison the moment Devon had closed the door behind him.

"I'm afraid my suspicions are becoming more and more valid each time."

"About Byrum and Sarah?" Harrison mentioned Markus's parents.

"Yes," Easton said. "I'm more and more convinced that Markus had something to do with their deaths.''

Easton paused. ''Even if he didn't do the deed personally, I'm sure he or Rademacher instigated it. Byrum was much too safe a driver to have a questionable Jeep accident.'' Easton leaned back. ''Frankly, I'm worried.''

''I understand. What can I do?''

''Marry my granddaughter Lucia and keep her safe,'' Easton said.

Chapter Fourteen

At the king's announcement Harrison bowed his head so Easton couldn't see the pain he was still in. He'd had the worst time of his life since Lucia's abrupt departure from Charlotte's apartment that day. "King Easton, I wish I could do what you just asked."

"You love my granddaughter."

"Yes." Harrison could not deny that. He'd spent days trying, and failing.

Easton took a sip of water. His hand shook as he placed the goblet back down. "So if you love her, what's the problem?"

"I told her about Mary."

"Ah." Easton leaned back as if he'd now seen the light. "Because of what I said in the heat of the moment, she still thinks you'd be marrying her out of a sense of duty, not because you love her."

"Exactly." Harrison nodded and clasped his hands together.

"Then you must convince her otherwise," Easton said as if that was the simplest thing in the world.

"I can't do that," Harrison pointed out. "You ordered me to stay away."

"Then I rescind the order," Easton said easily as if that made all the obstacles vanish. "I'm king. I can do that."

A bit of hope spread through Harrison when he realized that the king was serious. "You can, but why would you? You've now got your heir. You should be happy."

"Perhaps it's time for you to be happy." Easton tapped the tips of his fingers together. "You've given me many fine years, Harrison. Perhaps it's time to give yourself some fine years as well."

"My duty…" Harrison began, but before he could finish, Easton cut him off.

"Your duty is to be with the woman you love, even if she is going to be a queen. Being with the woman you love is the most important duty. I just forgot that fact for a little while. I've had the love of my life, and if Cassandra could have been here she would have told you the same thing. In fact, she probably would have made me see things a little more clearly a lot earlier."

"You're certain?" Harrison asked, his voice sounding more hopeful and alive than it had in days.

"Yes, I am." Easton smiled. Now all the issues burdening his soul had vanished. Well, he still had to deal with the disease, but right now he couldn't worry about that.

No one lived forever, and he'd had a wonderfully long life. When he finally did succumb to the disease, he would leave this world and join his beloved Cassandra, knowing that everything in Korosol was in good hands. Harrison and Lucia would see to it.

"You have only about six hours before the press conference," Easton said. "Go to her. Convince her that you love her. Tell her you'll make her happy. You will, I know, make her very happy."

"Thank you, Your Grace." Harrison stood, anxious to be immediately on his way.

"Harrison."

Harrison turned back around. "We're about to be family," Easton told him. "There are two requirements to that."

Harrison paused before executing his bow. "Yes?"

"One is stop the infernal bowing. The second is call me Easton and not Your Grace."

"But it's not proper," Harrison began. Easton cut him off.

"It is proper when you're both friends and family." Easton saw Harrison smile. "Go."

Easton watched Harrison rush out the door and

sat down. For the first time in a long time, a rare contentment filled him.

He leaned back and looked at the Manhattan skyline. The New York day was sunny, and a rare hope spread through him.

While he knew he still had to deal with Markus and Rademacher, he'd never planned on staying in New York this long. But one situation after another had laid claim to him, keeping him from his beloved Korosolan home.

Until now. Now, crisis averted, the problem of finding an heir to the throne was finally solved. He could deal with Markus tomorrow. Today he was happy that finally he could make plans to go home.

"WHAT DO YOU MEAN she's giving the press conference?" Markus's hand shook as he grabbed his scotch. "She's being named his heir?"

He listened for another moment and then slammed the secure line down. "My source at the embassy says Lucia is holding a press conference this afternoon. Security is so tight it can only mean one thing. Easton is naming her his heir."

"I don't believe it," Winston said. "I thought she was out of the picture. We need plan B."

"Exactly. Luckily for us I sent her that dress. At least our backup plan is in place," Markus said.

"You have impeccable foresight," Winston agreed.

"You bet I do," Markus said. He drank the remaining liquid in one gulp. "She cannot be allowed to rule. This throne is my birthright, not hers. I'm too close to my goal now. I will not allow some female American cousin who has only stepped foot in the country once to get my birthright. She cannot run Korosol."

"It wouldn't be a good idea," Winston agreed. "Easton should have named you his heir."

Markus broke a pencil in half. "He still will. He still will."

"MISS CARRADIGNE?"

Lucia picked up the in-house receiver. The doorman had just buzzed. She frowned. Now who was bothering her? Couldn't they all just leave her alone? She needed time, her own time, to recover. Besides, hadn't she just agreed to do what they wanted?

She'd agreed to be queen.

"Yes, Frank? What is it now?"

Poor Frank. She could tell by his tone this person had been even more difficult to deal with than her mother had been.

"Miss Carradigne," he said, "there's a gentleman here in the lobby and I can't get him to go away. I told him you didn't want to be disturbed and that I'd call the police if he didn't leave. Do you know that he laughed at me? He said he has diplomatic immunity.''

Lucia's forehead puckered. She wasn't expecting anyone. ''Did he tell you his name?''

''It's Harrison, Lucia.'' Lucia almost dropped the phone upon hearing Harrison's voice shouting in the background. ''Let me up.''

''Why?'' Lucia asked, her chin lifting stubbornly. The last thing she needed to do right now was see Harrison. She didn't need anything to test her new resolve to become queen.

His voice came clearly through the receiver, as if Frank had passed it over to him. ''Lucia, we need to talk. Let me up.''

She twirled the cord around her finger. How to answer that? Part of her so wanted to hear what he had to say, but she knew that would not be a wise idea. ''We have nothing to talk about.''

''Look, Lucia.'' At his tone, Lucia sensed Harrison's mounting frustration. ''If I have to, I'll climb the stairs and break down your fire door to see you.''

Lucia knew Harrison was deadly serious in what he intended to do. Plus, while the police might tote him away for a while, Lucia knew Harrison would just be right back harassing Frank within the hour.

He left her little choice. She certainly didn't want the police called to her building. She never would embarrass Harrison like that. Even though she had to let him go, she loved him too much to ever hurt him by damaging his reputation.

"I'm sending down the elevator," she said, although she really didn't want to face him. Dealing with a throng of reporters would be easier, and that task she had to do later today. It wasn't appealing either.

"Thank you," Frank said, and Lucia could hear the relief in the doorman's voice. Harrison had probably intimidated the diminutive doorman a great deal.

"No problem," Lucia said, praying her words were true.

Her instinct told her that letting Harrison up to her loft could be a problem, probably a big one. Her heart still hadn't healed.

Mentally she prepared herself.

This time she would be ready to greet him when he stepped off the elevator. She'd dressed for the press conference right after she'd made the phone call to the embassy.

Her mother would have advised against sitting around in her beautiful lime-green linen suit, but Lucia didn't care. She'd been ready for hours because that way she felt as if this change to her life was really happening. In a little less than five hours she would be named future queen of Korosol.

The elevator arrived and Harrison strode out. Catherine the Great, Lucia reminded herself. She could do this. She could face the life she'd chosen, the life without Harrison.

He stepped into view.

For the first time in over a week she saw him. He seemed haggard, as if he'd had sleepless nights. How her heart went out to him. She wanted to trace his eyebrows, caress his lips with her fingers until the pain in his eyes went away.

"Hello, Harrison," was all she said.

Chapter Fifteen

When he stepped off the elevator, that moment he first saw her again, Harrison had to contain himself.

His first instinct made him want to rush right up to her, take her into his arms, tell her he loved her and then kiss her absolutely senseless.

But from her cool, contained posture he knew he'd have to avoid that direct approach.

"Hello, Lucia," he said. "You look lovely."

She smoothed out an imaginary wrinkle in her skirt. "Thank you. You're looking well yourself."

"Well, I'm not," he said. "Well, that is."

Lucia's concern was immediate and Harrison felt a glimmer of hope. She still cared, at least a little. "You're ill?" she asked.

"You could say that," Harrison replied. He moved into her personal space, coming to stand in front of her. "Do you mind if we sit down?"

"Oh. Oh yes." She gestured toward the sofa. "Where are my manners?"

"Your manners are fine. I'm the one who showed up unannounced."

"That you did," she said. She sat primly on the edge of the sofa as if not to further wrinkle her skirt. Harrison knew it was actually because she was trying to maintain control. "Are you going to tell me why you are here?"

"If you could bear with me, I'd like to take my time. It's a long story and it takes some explaining," Harrison said, taking a seat as close to her as he dared. He put his hands on his knees.

Lucia shrugged, but the hair she'd wrapped up into a tight French knot didn't budge an inch. She'd even tucked up the ringlets. "Suit yourself, Harrison. Just know that I have to be at the embassy at three-thirty."

"I know that," he said.

"Is that why you're here? My grandfather did let you keep your job, didn't he?"

"Lucia, please. Yes, he did, but please let me tell this my way."

"Sorry." She looked so put out that for a moment Harrison wanted nothing more than to kiss her.

"Don't be sorry. Just let me talk. I have so much I want to tell you." He drew a deep, steadying breath. "I've told you all about Mary, and the reasons why I married her."

"Yes." Lucia nodded.

"I was faithful to Mary even though we were estranged. She, however, had met someone else and would have divorced me if she hadn't contracted pneumonia and died. While there have been one or two other women I dated after her death, I didn't ever love any of them. My duty to Korosol always came first."

"That reminds me." Lucia bounded to her feet. She moved quickly to her workbench and returned with a small box. "This is ready. I made it for you."

Her fingers connected with his palm as she placed the tiny paper box in his hand. Harrison's own trembled as he removed the white lid. Inside was a tiny burgundy-colored box, and inside that, on black velvet, sat the tie tack.

Harrison's heart shattered into pieces. She had finished the piece she had been working on. It was a perfect Korosolan symbol of honor.

"I wanted you to always know how I felt," she said. "You've been like Gregory Peck's character in *Roman Holiday*."

"I never saw that movie either," Harrison said. He made a mental note to make sure they watched it together someday way in the future. Right now he needed to convince her they belonged together.

"He was a reporter," she told him. "He found a princess who had escaped her royal life. He gave her the freedom she craved. In the end he kept her secret and let her go. Anyway, that's what you did for me. Thank you for giving me one last week of freedom, one last week of happiness.''

"Lucia, I—''

"Please, let me finish,'' her soft voice pleaded.

Harrison wondered how he'd lost control of the conversation but decided it didn't matter. He'd let her talk, get all her arguments out in the open. Then he'd defeat them, just as she had defeated all his protests back in Aspen.

She gripped the hem of her skirt. "I know what I'm doing. I choose, under my own free will, to become queen. I'm ready to leave this part of my life behind. You've taught me some things, you know, and one of them is that I can't shirk from doing my duty.''

Watching her further broke Harrison's heart. He closed the burgundy-colored jeweler's box and slid it into his pocket.

"You will make a fine queen,'' he said. "No one is prouder of you than me.''

"It will be hard for me, knowing I can't see you, but it would be harder for me to know that I caused you to lose the job you loved,'' Lucia said.

"You haven't cost me my job,'' Harrison said. "But I'm thinking of retiring anyway. I have been doing this a long time.''

"You can't.''

"What?'' He looked confused.

"Retire! You can't retire. Not on my account."

"On your account," he repeated, trying to understand. He saw her stricken face and immediately knew she was blaming herself. "Lucia, listen to me. My career means nothing if it means I can't have you."

She paced the room. "You must not say things like that. I don't believe you. Your career means everything to you!"

Harrison stood and went over to stand by her. He placed both hands on her shoulders. "Listen to me. You mean everything. That's what I came over here to tell you."

She tried to pull back but he wouldn't let her. "Lucia, I've fallen in love with you. You. Not the future queen of Korosol. I know I'm not the right man for you."

She opened her mouth and he rushed on. "Let me finish," he said.

"Okay," she said.

Harrison began again. "Lucia, I've been wrestling with my heart. I'm too old, too jaded in this modern world. But in the end I had to admit one thing to myself."

He paused, and Lucia waited. "Lucia, I love you, and I want to spend the rest of my life with you. If that means retiring from service to become prince consort and be with you, then I'll do it. I'd love you if you were a pauper and I was the richest man in the world. I want you that much.''

"You love me.'' She repeated his declaration and Harrison saw the first light of hope dawn in her beautiful green eyes.

"Yes,'' he said with a nod. His hazel eyes darkened. "I love you more than my job, more than life itself. It would never be a duty to stand right next to you and be at your side. It would be a labor of love. Don't you know that your love makes me the richest man in the world? It makes me complete, whole, in a way my job never has. Lucia, I love you.''

"Oh, Harrison!'' Lucia threw her arms around his neck and let the tears flow freely. Harrison never thought he would see a lovelier sight than his Lucia weeping from happiness.

"Lucia, darling, don't cry.'' He took a handkerchief from his pocket.

"You love me,'' she repeated. Her tears mixed with a sob of pure joy.

"Absolutely and truly,'' he said. He kissed her forehead and began to wipe away her tears.

"You've just made my dreams come true. Do you know how much I love you?'' Her green eyes glistened, revealing the full extent of her love.

He smiled. "If you love me even half as much as I love you then it is more than enough,'' he said.

He inhaled her essence. Her hair smelled of roses. He'd never smelled anything sweeter.

Knowing he'd awaken every day for the rest of his life to his perfect rose made him the happiest man in the entire world.

"Oh, I love you more than that," she said. She wiped her face with her right forefinger. She looked at the black smear from her runny mascara. "Oh, I can't believe it. Look at me! I'm a mess."

"I've never seen you more beautiful," he said truthfully. He wiped her finger with the handkerchief. "You've become my life, Lucia, and I can't imagine spending another minute without you being by my side."

"So stay with me," she said.

"That's my line," he replied with a small chuckle. "Don't steal all of them. I want to do this right."

He reached into his pocket and withdrew a burgundy-colored jeweler's box. "Wrong one," he said. He reached again. The one he withdrew this time was black.

"I picked this up on my way here," he said, opening the box to reveal an engagement ring. "It's not as fancy as the jewelry you make, but..."

"But it's perfect," Lucia said. She was already reaching for it.

"You are going to let me get the words out, aren't you?" he teased. "I never said them to Mary.

It was sort of dictated by her father that we'd wed, and I agreed. I'd like to say the words to you."

Tears brimmed in Lucia's eyes. "Sorry. I'm just so excited, so happy. I just love you so much, and this is the best day of my life. I thought we'd never get to be together again."

"Shh, and stop saying sorry," Harrison said. "You have nothing to be sorry about. I love your impulsivity. I love your commitment to your work. I love you, and can't imagine my life without you. Will you marry me, Lucia? Will you be my wife and stay with me until the end of time?"

"Yes," Lucia said. Her fingers trembled in his as he slid the ring onto the third finger of her left hand. She gazed at the simple solitaire in the plain band of gold. Coming from the heart, it was the most beautiful piece of jewelry she'd ever seen.

Harrison loved her. She could see it in his eyes. She repeated her joy. "Yes, I would be honored to call myself your wife."

"Then seal it with a kiss," he teased, and lowered his mouth to hers.

"Yes," she said as his lips connected with hers. Heaven waited, and there was nothing she wanted more than to be back reunited physically with the man she loved. "Oh yes."

She pulled his head down, and Harrison felt the urgency flow between them. Lucia was already pulling at the buttons of his shirt. "I need you now," she told him without preamble.

And she did.

They kissed all the way to Lucia's bed. Harrison placed her tenderly upon it. "I love you," he told her.

"I love you," Lucia replied, and then silenced him with another kiss.

Upon their joining, Harrison felt her detonate immediately.

Later, snuggling in Lucia's bed, Harrison glanced at his watch. He bolted straight up.

"What is it?" she asked.

"We have to be at the embassy."

"We have over two hours," Lucia said. She stretched languorously.

"But we need to tell Easton what we've decided."

Lucia sat up, the sheet falling lower. Harrison wondered if he'd ever get used to the sight of Lucia's beauty, and knew he never would. Each day with her would be a treasure.

"You are right," Lucia agreed. "But what have we decided?"

"To get married." He traced her nose with his forefinger.

"Besides that." She playfully slapped his hand away, and it landed somewhere else lower.

"I guess we do need to decide when and where,"

Harrison said, stroking Lucia's inner thigh through the sheet.

Lucia nodded. "I'd actually like to get married as fast as it can be arranged. That way Grandfather will get what he wants."

"Then that's what we'll tell him," Harrison said, using a forefinger to trace her shoulder blade.

"Later," Lucia said, and she drew his lips back down toward hers.

"YOU'RE SURE?" Easton asked. He stared at his granddaughter.

"Positive," Lucia said.

"I can't convince you to change your mind?"

"No." Lucia put her arms around Harrison and gazed at the man she loved. "I'm sorry to disappoint you, but I don't think I should take the crown. All I want is a quiet life with Harrison."

"I understand," Easton said. He hid his disappointment. He'd so hoped he'd just found the perfect royal couple for his beloved homeland.

"We'll divide our time between Korosol and New York," Lucia continued, "but we want to start a family as soon as possible."

"I'm not getting any younger," Harrison joked. Easton could see the love flow between his granddaughter and his friend. They would be happy, just as he and his dear Cassandra had been.

"But, it concerns me, what will you do?" Lucia asked.

"Not pick Markus," Easton said. Lucia frowned, and Easton remembered she didn't know any of his or Harrison's suspicions. "My middle son, James, had three wives. With two of them he fathered four sons. I'm headed to Wyoming next to meet my grandsons and see if one of them has the potential to be my heir."

"You haven't seen much of James for over thirty years," Harrison pointed out.

"No." Easton sighed. "He left Korosol to pursue his dreams, and it's long past time for me to reconnect with my son. You know, I have no idea what those dreams of his were."

A knock on the door announced Ellie's arrival into Easton's office.

"I've canceled the press conference," she said. "I've also arranged for a minister and a small private ceremony at Charlotte's apartment the day after tomorrow. Princess Lucia, your mother told me to tell you that she's thrilled, and would like to talk to you when you have a minute to call her."

"Thank you," Lucia said.

"I've also spoken with Sir Devon," Ellie continued. "He relays his congratulations and said he will get right on the security arrangements."

"Good," Easton said. He wondered how he

would ever manage without Ellie. She was so efficient. He hoped she liked Wyoming.

Easton turned to Lucia and gave his granddaughter a smile. "Think two days is enough time?"

"It's way too long," she said. She held on to Harrison, and Easton saw love radiating from every pore. "But I think I'll survive the wait as long as this man is my husband."

"I always will be," Harrison promised, and Easton smiled. He knew his granddaughter was in good hands.

He just wished Korosol's future was the same.

Epilogue

"You are so sweet to help me pack for my trip and close up my apartment," Lucia said two days later.

"Think nothing of it," Ellie replied. "It got me out of the embassy for a while. By the way, I love your loft."

"Thanks," Lucia said. She tossed her bikini into a suitcase. She and Harrison had been married three hours ago on her mother's terrace overlooking Central Park. The New York sky had been clear and sunny, and the weather absolutely perfect for being outside.

She was now Mrs. Harrison Montcalm, and she couldn't have been happier.

"So where are you going again?" Ellie asked. She closed one of Lucia's suitcases.

"After a month in the Western Caribbean we're headed to Korosol. I was a little girl when I was there last, and after all the fuss, I'm ready to see it again." Lucia paused, studying her loft.

Had she forgotten anything? She'd given her plants to Charles's fiancée, Amy, so that item was taken care of. She glanced at the list Harrison had created for her. She only had one item left to do, the one that said, "Leave with your husband on a honeymoon because he plans to love you for the rest of your life."

"That sounds wonderful," Ellie said as she read the last item on the list.

"Being anywhere with Harrison is wonderful," Lucia admitted.

Her gaze suddenly landed on the box that Markus had sent a while ago. Ellie had told her he'd been out of town when she'd tried to contact him about the canceled press conference. Lucia didn't know if her cousin Markus even knew about her sudden wedding.

"Have you had any fun at all this trip?" Lucia asked.

The question came out of the blue, and Ellie blinked. "Huh?" she replied.

"Fun," Lucia said. "Have you even seen anything of New York?"

Ellie paused, and then shook her head. "No. I thought I would, but it hasn't turned out that way. Oh, please don't take it the wrong way. My job isn't to have fun. I don't want it to sound like I'm complaining. I just thought I would get out a few more times."

Lucia nodded. "Well, I have a solution. Why don't you take this?"

Ellie straightened and Lucia pressed her personal invitation to the Inferno Ball into Ellie's hand. "A ball?" Ellie asked.

"It's the event of the season. Come on, you just told me you haven't had any real fun since you've been here. Perhaps you'll meet someone."

"I won't worry about that," Ellie said with a blush. "It'll just be fun to get out. I have been confined pretty much to the embassy."

"Well, you need to go to this. Seriously. Use my invitation and get a good seat for the charity auction. It's a lot of fun, and you'll meet some of Manhattan's most eligible men."

"You are so sweet, Princess, but I really don't have anything to wear."

"Let me tell you a little secret, Ellie. If you want something, you need to make it happen. Now let's see. You're about my size. This should do."

Lucia passed over the fire-red gown Markus had sent her. "I'd give you another, but I never clean them until right before I need them. It's a habit that drove my mother crazy when I lived at home."

"Really, this is too much," Ellie protested. "You've already been more than kind by just giving me the invitation."

"Actually, you need jewelry to go with it." Lucia ignored Ellie's protests. She went over to her workbench and grabbed some pieces. "These will be perfect. They'll make your ears look delicate."

A buzz told her the elevator was on its way up. "We're here!" her sisters chorused as they arrived.

Amelia smiled and hugged Lucia. "It's time to take you back to the embassy to meet your husband. It's honeymoon time!"

CeCe patted her ever-growing belly. "I know how mine went," she said. "My husband discovered he couldn't live without me."

"I am ready," Lucia said. She was. Harrison was her future, and she was ready to get started. She glanced around her loft one last time. Leaving home for part of the year didn't seem so bad when she knew Harrison would be with her. He was her home, her hope, her future.

"Then let's go." CeCe led the way.

"TAKE CARE of yourself," Harrison told King Easton hours later as everyone stood on the heliport of Charlotte's apartment building.

Easton nodded at his trusted adviser, and now a member of his family. It had been a wonderful evening. Once Lucia and her sisters had arrived, the entire family, minus Markus, had gathered for one last dinner before Easton headed to Wyoming, and Harrison and Lucia to the Western Caribbean for their honeymoon.

Devon approached him. "The helicopter awaits," he told Easton. "Anytime you are ready we can depart."

Easton nodded. Time to head out to Wyoming. He had an heir to find. Ellie would follow him tomorrow, after she attended a ball tonight and tied up some loose ends at the embassy the next day.

He glanced at the helicopter that would take him to the airport. It was hard leaving Harrison behind, but it was time for goodbyes. "You take care of your wife," Easton told him.

"I will," Harrison said. Both men watched Lucia come toward them. "Good luck with your search."

"I need it," Easton said. He suddenly reached forward and gave Harrison a firm handshake. "You're a good man, Harrison. I'm glad to call you family."

"Thanks, Easton." Harrison tried out the familiar use of Easton's name.

The king turned as Devon approached again. "Is there a problem with takeoff?"

Devon coughed as if not sure to speak in front of the entire family. "No, but we have another problem."

The entire family turned their gazes toward him. "Speak," Easton said.

"It seems as though Eleanor Standish has been kidnapped," Devon said. "The embassy staff received a ransom note just a few minutes ago. In the note the kidnappers described the red dress she was wearing to the Inferno Ball."

"That was my dress!" Lucia exclaimed.

"Exactly," Devon said. "The kidnappers think she's you."

Lucia swayed against Harrison, and Easton stepped forward. "Come, Devon. Let's let everyone else go home." He turned to his family. There was Charlotte, CeCe and Shane, Amelia and Nick, Harrison and Lucia. Nick's face was ashen. Ellie was his sister. "There's nothing you can do. Please go on home. I know it's hard, but Devon and I will handle this. Nick, I promise we'll find her. We'll do whatever it takes."

Although they didn't want to, the family began to file back to the elevator that would take them to their respective cars.

"That was to be me," Lucia said. Harrison tightened his grip around her shoulders. Immediately she felt comforted.

"I'm glad it's not," Harrison said.

"Are you sad to be missing the action?" Lucia asked Harrison.

Harrison turned to her. "For a second, I was. Then I thought, this is Devon's time. Then, even better, I remembered that I love you, and you are everything I've ever wanted. But we will have to postpone our trip to the Caribbean until they catch whoever wanted to kidnap you, and Ellie is safe."

"So I guess we are both going to miss the action," Lucia said wryly, but realized that the postponement of the honeymoon was for the best.

"I am not going to miss the action of seducing my wife in a secret hideaway in New York until this all blows over," Harrison said watching Lucia's face brighten.

His wife. He liked the idea. He'd chosen Lucia because he loved her, not because of duty. He looked forward to this marriage, and the happiness that he knew would exist with him the rest of his days.

"Then, my darling husband, I'd say we get on with it," Lucia said.

She kissed him, and Harrison felt contentment fill him. His Lucia loved him, and that made him the richest man in the world.

"Follow me, my lady," he said. "Follow me."

* * * * *

What will happen to Ellie Standish?
Find out in

THE DUKE'S COVERT MISSION

by Julie Miller

Coming next month from
Harlequin Intrigue.

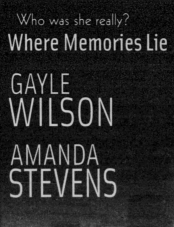

Brides of
the
DESERT ROSE

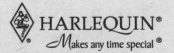